DINOSAUR GEORGE and the PALEONAUTS

EPISODE ONE: RAPTOR ISLAND

George Blasing & Mark Miller

Cover design and illustration by Gabriel Bush

First Edition

Published by
Dinosaur George Media

ISBN: 978-0615938776

Printed in the United States of America

CHAPTER ONE

"How big do you think this thing is?" asked George. He did not want his excitement to get the better of him on his first dig.

Professor Evert Stone pushed his hat back on his head. The wide brim kept the muggy Florida sun out of his face. The field crew stayed busy while Professor Stone supervised with George at his side. Stone said, "It's not a record breaker, if that's what you're asking."

George knew dinosaurs. He loved dinosaurs. For all eighteen years of his young life, he studied dinosaurs. He studied everything prehistoric and that included mammoths. As soon as George got his high school diploma, he volunteered for an internship with his uncle, Professor Stone, to help him prepare for college. It happened to be the most fun summer of his life.

With only a few weeks to the start of his first semester of college, George went with Professor Stone to Florida to excavate a recently exposed fossil. A horse rancher was plowing one of his fields to make way for a bank of solar panels. It amused George that the rancher was about to become a sun farmer too. Because Florida was under water during the time of the dinosaurs, the state was known more for its ice age relics and creatures.

As one of the leading experts in the country, Professor Stone came to oversee the dig. The rancher suspected he did not uncover some ordinary rock. The Professor confirmed it was a fossil, the upper thigh bone of a mammoth to be precise.

George and the Professor stood in the shade of a moss covered oak tree. George grew up in San Antonio, Texas and he thought he knew hot. However, he discovered August in Florida is its own special kind of hot. He did not know his ears could sweat until now.

While they waited for the crew to finish the final dusting, the camera crew set up on a platform to take wide angle pictures of the whole site. A jeep came roaring across the pasture as if it was an extension of the nearby interstate. A young man, George guessed not much older than himself, jumped out from behind the steering wheel. He looked like a marine with a buzz cut and near perfect posture. George was raised to have great respect for the men and women of his country's military.

The soldier walked directly toward Professor Stone. He did not seem to be interested in the almost complete mammoth fossil sticking out of the ground.

"Professor Stone?" asked the man.

"Please call me Evert," said the Professor.

The young man did not smile or move. He said, "Professor Stone, I am Vince Witmer, head of security for Dr. Joseph Morgan."

Professor Stone started to laugh. George joined in, but did not know why. The Professor said, "How is the old egg-head? I haven't seen him in years."

Vince did not crack a smile. George wondered if he had his funny bone removed. Vince looked to be in his mid-twenties, but he acted like an old soldier.

"Dr. Morgan has made a recent discovery and has specifically requested your presence," said Vince.

Professor Stone removed his dusty, old hat and wiped his forehead with his lucky handkerchief. The white square of cloth usually hung out from the pocket on the front left of his shirt. "This could be interesting," said the Professor.

Vince headed back to the jeep. He stopped when he saw Professor Stone was not following him. Vince said, "Professor, I am to take you to him immediately. I have a helicopter waiting."

The Professor dropped his hat back on his head and smiled at George. He said, "Get in the jeep, boy."

Vince made a small cough, like he was clearing his throat. "Only you, sir, unless his name is George. Dr.

Morgan said I was to look for someone named George, too."

Professor Stone stood next to Vince and put a hand on his shoulder. He said, "George is my nephew and he is also my brightest student. He is a dinosaur prodigy. Even if his name was Henry, he would still be coming."

It took Professor Stone a few minutes to arrange things with one of the other field assistants. Soon after, the jeep bounced back across the field. George watched out the open back as the photographer climbed up on the platform to take pictures of the long buried mammoth.

George had only ridden in a helicopter once before during a Snake River sightseeing trip. He had never flown in one cross-country. The helicopter left the small regional airfield in Florida and did not stop until it had to refuel in Saint Louis. From there, Vince piloted the helicopter north. George thought a jet would have been faster, but he enjoyed watching the farms and houses pass beneath them. He tried to pick out landmarks and cities as they went. The Mississippi River was unmistakably wide and the hills surrounding Mount Rushmore looked amazing.

George knew a famous dinosaur institute situated in the Black Hills and asked Vince through the headset if that was where they were going.

"I'm sorry, but I cannot tell you the exact location. Dr. Morgan is not working with the institute on this project.

Please put on the blindfolds for the final leg of the trip," said Vince.

It made George nervous, but his uncle put on his blindfold with a grin. The Professor always seemed to have a sense of adventure and fun. Not long after, Vince landed the helicopter. George did not see where they landed, but he knew it still had to be in South Dakota.

Vince took their blindfolds and then led them to a pair of large metal doors that looked like they grew out of the side of the reddish-brown mountain rock. Tall evergreens and broadleaf trees, totally different than those in Florida, surrounded the small helicopter clearing. George could not hear any car traffic. Only the sound of a nearby wood duck greeted them.

Professor Stone looked at the impressive door and said, "Either Dr. Morgan finally got his grant money or he joined Doomsday Preppers."

Vince still did not laugh. He walked over to the side of the door and lifted a rock. The false stone was actually a cover for the door controls. Vince spoke into a tiny microphone, "ID T-R-X-6-1-7-3."

The big metal doors started to open. George imagined steam creeping out from behind the doors.

Instead of smoke and insects, a long white hall waited for them. Vince led George and his uncle deep into the mountain. At the end of the hall, they came to another door. It did not look as imposing to George. Before Vince could open it, a man in a white lab coat came through from the other side.

"Nice to see you, Evert. What took you so long to get here?" asked the man.

"Very funny, Joseph," Professor Stone replied. "I think Vince got us here as fast as he could." He turned to present George. "Dr. Joseph Morgan, this is my nephew and future student. He starts college in a couple weeks and will be one of my star pupils."

"You are in for quite a treat, young man," said Dr. Morgan to George.

He opened the door and they entered a huge cave. Lights had been hung from wires stretched over their heads. Makeshift offices had been setup at one end, the kind with only walls and no ceilings. People looked busy at various workstations setup throughout the enormous cave. George thought it was the neatest secret lab he had ever seen. He said, "This is better than the Batcave."

"There will be time for a tour later. I have something to discuss with you both that is quite urgent," said Dr. Morgan. He took them to the only completely private office in the cave. It even had a ceiling and sound proof walls. Vince followed them, but stopped right outside the door. Apparently, he was not allowed to hear what Dr. Morgan had to say.

Even with the door closed, Dr. Morgan spoke almost in a whisper. He said, "I don't know where to begin. I have two things to show you and I think they are connected. Maybe I will start with this."

He entered his password on his computer. George could not see what Dr. Morgan typed, but he knew it had to be at least thirty characters long. Who has a password that long, he wondered.

Dr. Morgan clicked on one of only two files on the computer desktop. It contained an audio file. As it loaded, he said, "This is the reason we are here."

It only lasted a few seconds, but George had no mistake at whose voice he heard. The voice of his uncle, Professor Evert Stone seemed to come to him from a million miles away. He said, "Joseph, it worked. Are you happy? George, whatever you do…"

The recording stopped.

"Is that it?" asked George. He wanted to jump up and down to hear more. "What worked? What am I supposed to do?"

George looked to his uncle. The Professor looked clueless. He said, "George, I never made a recording like that. What's the joke, Joseph?"

Dr. Morgan stood from his desk. He said, "It is no joke. I have an idea of its origin and that brings me to the other reason why we are here. It's taken us a long time to get to this point, but we have actually perfected time travel."

"No way!" exclaimed George.

Professor Stone only smiled. He slapped Dr. Morgan on his back and said, "If anyone could do it, I knew it would be you. That's all you've talked about for twenty years. Are you going to show us how you did it?"

Dr. Morgan explained some highly technical things as they walked from his office. Vince followed them closely. George still could not believe what he was hearing. If what

Dr. Morgan said was true, the possibilities could be endless. He felt overwhelmed, but his uncle looked calm. At the back of the cave, George could see several vehicles, but they stopped in front of something that looked like a giant soccer goal with wires running from both posts to countless computers. Security barriers surrounded the area to keep people at least ten feet away on all sides.

Dr. Morgan nodded to a young woman with pink stripes in her blond hair. She began flipping switches and pushing buttons. George could feel an electric field generate around the *soccer goal*. The short hairs on his arms and legs stood on end, but he could not see anything change.

"Evert, have a look at this radio," said Dr. Morgan. "It is one of our earliest prototypes. I think you will find that this is what made the recording on my computer."

George did not understand what was happening, but it looked like his uncle did.

"This is going to be your first human test, isn't it?" asked Professor Stone.

"I'm afraid it is the only way possible to set events in motion," answered Dr. Morgan.

Professor Stone turned on the radio. A blue-green-purple sheet of energy snapped alive between the posts. Before George knew what was happening, Dr. Morgan pushed Professor Stone into the field. George's uncle disappeared before his eyes.

"No!" yelled George. "Bring him back." Vince grabbed George before he could run into the field. He realized he would probably be disintegrated too, but he wanted to try and help his uncle.

"This is not the way to help him," said Dr. Morgan. "We have much to discuss and many more recordings to listen to."

It took George some time to calm down. He sat in Dr. Morgan's office, worried about his uncle.

Dr. Morgan said, "George, there are two things you have to learn about time travel. Causality and Paradox. I have so many more recordings, but for these two reasons, I cannot let you hear all of them."

He turned his computer monitor toward George. George watched him click on the second folder. Instead of only one file like the first folder, it contained hundreds. Dr. Morgan sorted through the files for a moment and found the one he wanted to play.

"George, listen to me," spoke his uncle. This recording of Professor Stone sounded as equally distant as the first. "I'm okay. Don't worry. I think Dr. Morgan has some bugs to fix in his time machine. I keep jumping to different eras. It takes all my skills, but I am surviving. I think the battery on this radio is finally dying. I hope these messages help you. Maybe you don't feel like it, but you can trust Dr. Morgan."

The Professor was right. George did not feel like he could trust Dr. Morgan. However, if his uncle told him he could, then he would at least try.

Dr. Morgan turned off his monitor and looked at George. He said, "I have been receiving these messages for years. I recognized Evert Stone's voice, but I did not know who George was until today when I met you. Your uncle is randomly jumping through time. I think we have solved that problem and I would like you to lead the team to try and bring him back."

Me, George asked himself. He started to say, "I don't have the qualifications…"

"You will have the best team and finest equipment. I can't let you hear all the recordings, but trust me when I say, you are the only one for the job."

Dr. Morgan led the way back out into the laboratory cave. George saw Vince driving a huge vehicle that sort of resembled a motor home up to the time travel soccer goal. It kind of looked like a spaceship on super-durable wheels.

"What is that?" asked George.

"That is your command center vehicle," replied the doctor. "We call it the Land Vehicle One, or LV1 for short." The LV1 had to be longer than a city bus. From the wide observation windows on the side, George could see it was equipped with monitors, radios, computers and an array of other high-tech gear.

Dr. Morgan continued, "In the rear of the LV1 is the EB5, or Exo-Bouncer 5. Picture it as an armored SUV with all of the latest upgrades from the Mars Manned Mission project. That's your recon unit. It is a two-person vehicle with an on-board Sub-Cycle. The Sub-Cycle is both a mini-submarine and motorcycle."

George looked at all of the amazing equipment. He said, "You guys thought of everything, but I have one question. If that is the EB5, what happened to versions one through four?"

Vince leaned out the driver's window of the LV1. He said, "You don't want to know."

The pink haired girl came over to show Dr. Morgan something on her tablet. He tapped a few icons and then she stepped back. He said, "Thank you, Parker. George, this is Parker Holtz, our computer specialist. You already know Vince, our head of security and LV1 pilot." Dr. Morgan pointed behind George. "These two joining us now are your chief medic and engineer, Sonya Currie and Lloyd Lance, respectively."

Sonya looked kind, but George thought Lloyd did not have a clue where he was. The older man had a wild beard and thick braided hair. He looked like a skinny version of the giant in that boy wizard story George read once.

"Nice to meet you, monsieur," said Sonya with a French accent. With her dark skin, George guessed she had to be from the Caribbean. He liked the way she talked and extended his hand in greeting.

Sonya would not shake. She said, "I do no shake hands."

Lloyd stuck out his greasy hand instead. He started rapidly shaking George's hand before George could pull away. "Sorry about that man. Like I was tuning up the

EB5. Sonya doesn't shake hands man. She's one of those, you know, germaphobes."

"But she's the doctor, isn't she?" asked George.

"And the best in her field," added Dr. Morgan. "You have an elite team and I have a schedule to keep. New recordings keep coming in from the past, but we have not figured out a way to send messages back. From the time table I put together, we have about three weeks before you make your first mission. There is a lot of training to do until then."

Lloyd finally let go of George's hand and gave him a big hug. "This is so cool man. We get to work with *the* Dinosaur George."

Parker threw her stylus at Lloyd. She said, "Way to go Lloyd. He doesn't call himself that yet."

Dinosaur George. Eighteen year old George liked the sound of that nickname. It sounded like the name of a great adventurer. He did not feel like an adventurer though. He felt a little scared and had some doubt. He did not think Professor Stone would feel like this. He wished he could be more like his uncle. George could not imagine anybody really calling him by that nickname.

He spent the next three weeks learning everything he could about all of the high-tech tools, gadgets and vehicles that Dr. Morgan supplied. He learned to drive the EB5 and spent some time in the mini-sub. Lloyd called the mini-sub Princess Caroline, so George did too. He spent an entire day diving in the Olympic-sized swimming pool. Vince also gave George a brief introduction to their emergency gear: a combination hang-glider and jet pack as well as all of their non-lethal weaponry.

Parker gave George a brief overview of the time-travel components. He guessed they were about the same age and he really liked how she changed her hair color about once a week. Today, she dyed it dark green, almost the color of her eyes. George could not stop staring at her.

"Okay George, I think you're cute too, but we have work to do," said Parker. She winked at him and looked back at the console.

George felt his face burn three shades of red. He did think she was cute, but now he was too embarrassed to think anything else.

Finally, the day came to board the LV1 for their first mission. George climbed in with his team. Vince fired up the Hydrogen engine and Parker entered their geo-temporal coordinates. George discussed traveling to Asia during the late Cretaceous Period, but the secretive Dr. Morgan would not give him any more information. He only said, "Look around for your uncle. I don't think you will find him there, but we have to start somewhere. Take the opportunity to see some living dinosaurs. You could collect some invaluable data."

Inside the LV1, Parker explained, "Inside the Land Vehicle, we are tethered to *The Goal* (everyone started calling it that since George said it looked like a giant soccer goal). It is on an auto-return cycle of twenty-four hours. That way, we don't get lost in time."

She winked at George again. George could feel his cheeks go red. He turned around in his seat to find Vince staring at him. This only added to his embarrassment.

"Are we ready to go, love birds?" Vince asked.

This brought a big laugh from Lloyd and a caring smile from Sonya. Parker punched a couple buttons at her console like she was mad at Vince. She said, "All clear."

Vince pushed the throttle lever and the LV1 rolled through the shimmering *Goal*. The world outside the observation windows changed from the dark cave to a bright white, almost liquid atmosphere. In less than thirty seconds, the LV1 travelled back in time more than sixty-five million years.

CHAPTER TWO

The white light around the LV1 faded into a normal sunlit day. Still brighter than Dr. Morgan's lab, it took a moment for George's eyes to adjust. When he could see, it amazed him.

Lush green trees surrounded them. Out the side window, George could see singed leaves where they materialized and burned back the foliage. He saw no other signs of damage. George did not want to be responsible for starting a prehistoric forest fire. Vince steered the LV1 into a small grove.

"This should provide some cover," he said.

"From what?" asked George.

Vince looked worried. He glanced at Parker and she shrugged. He said, "Um, a meteor shower maybe."

George wondered if Vince was keeping a secret, but he had more important things to do. He wanted to explore this new, or old, world. He ran to the back of the LV1 to find Lloyd doing a system check on the Exo-Bouncer.

"It's all ready, little buddy," said Lloyd.

The driver's seat looked inviting. George wanted to jump in, but he saw the steering wheel on the passenger's side. It was reversed. Vince beat him to the actual driver's seat.

"I have my driver's license," said George.

"Sorry kid. It's my job."

Lloyd went to push a large red button on the back wall.

"Wait," shouted Sonya. George looked at her wearing a breathing mask and rubber gloves that went up to her elbows. "I need an air sample before you open that door."

As the doctor said this, the computer behind her started beeping. She checked the results of her air test. Then she opened an overhead cabinet and removed several vials.

Sonya said, "That's what I thought. We have one more inoculation to do. We don't want to introduce any new germs into the environment."

George liked needles about as much as he liked snakes. And that was NOT AT ALL. He already had enough shots during training to last him the rest of his life. After the latest shot, Lloyd finally opened the back door. The entire wall lowered like a medieval drawbridge and served as the ramp for Vince to back out the EB5. As soon as the vehicle cleared the ramp, Lloyd sealed the LV1. Vince punched a few buttons and the dark interior of the EB5 lit up with a bank of monitors. George did not need to try to peek out the narrow front windshield. He could see all around them with the tiny cameras mounted to the body of the EB5.

"Downlink confirmed," came Parker's voice. George forgot about his new watch. Well, it was not really a watch, or not *only*. The tiny touch screen device also monitored his life signs and worked as a remote control for the EB5, among other things. He could also use it to communicate with the LV1.

George held his wrist close to his mouth and said, "Roger."

"Whoa, not so loud, George," said Parker. "I can hear everything in a ten foot radius of your Chrono-Health-Remote-Meter."

"I thought we agreed to call it *C.H.R.M.* for short?" asked Vince. "As in, George is wearing his *Charm* bracelet."

Parker giggled. George tried to imagine her smile, but mostly he felt embarrassed by Vince's comment. Maybe Vince liked Parker too, he thought. George wanted to be mature, so he did not respond. Vince verified the uplink on their end. All of the EB5 sensors would be sending a constant stream of data to the two-petabyte hard drive on board the LV1.

The center console came to life with a 3-D navigation system. It projected a topographical map of the area created from long range sonar scans. It looked to George like they were close to a sheer cliff. Checking the monitor in front of him, he could only see a long stretch of beach and an island in the distance. He deduced that the ground must drop off suddenly below the surface of the water. The deeper it got, the bigger the sea creatures could get. He did not look forward to any swimming. Vince drove them down the beach until they could find a good opening into the jungle. They spotted a wide trail and turned into the woods, putting the beach behind them.

The forest looked empty. Not a living thing to be seen. Not even an insect. Did they end up in the wrong place or time, George wondered. They continued deeper into the forest in search of any signs of life. He hoped his uncle would be here somewhere.

After about twenty minutes, George said, "Let's stop here."

"You can't get out," said Vince. They had this discussion once before, during training. As head of security, Vince had to keep George safe. That meant not letting him out of the armored vehicle.

George could not resist. He wanted to breathe the air and feel the dirt. He wanted to hear the forest sounds, if there were any, with his own ears. They had been driving all this time and not seen a single animal. He pulled the lever to open his door and said, "What's the worst that could happen?"

His imagination barely came close to the real forest. Looking at it through the EB5 monitors, he knew there was no grass and hardly any plants growing on the forest floor. However, huge palm trees towered over him like Texas skyscrapers.

A deep rumble shattered the silence of the forest— almost like thunder, but not exactly. The sound came from further up the game trail that they had been following in the EB5. Off in the distance, to George's left, he heard a similar roar. Was it an echo of the first or really thunder moving across the sky?

Neither.

George had a feeling it was some *thing* calling out to another *thing*. Could it be a mate searching for its partner? Lost offspring calling for a parent? Or a herd member announcing a new food source? Regardless, George knew he was the first man in history to hear the sound of a dinosaur!

George's excitement overtook him. He raced into the jungle, leaving behind the safety of the EB5. As he ran, he wondered if the dinosaurs were herbivores or carnivores. George thought how great it would be to see a huge carnivore on his first journey back in time.

He slid to a stop. A carnivore! What was he thinking?

Instead of serving himself up as dinner, he turned back toward Vince and the EB5. George jumped into his seat and slammed the door. Although there was nothing chasing him, he could not help but think something was right behind him the entire way to the vehicle. His heart pounded and he realized Vince was laughing at him. As exciting as it was, George knew he could not risk being injured, or worse, eaten. He had to find his uncle. Seeing dinosaurs was secondary.

George regained his composure and asked, "Can we track that sound?"

The EB5 came fully equipped with a variety of tracking sensors. Vince hit a few more buttons and they could easily track motion, sound or by heat signatures. Even better, George knew they had excellent security features to protect them from almost anything. The best part about the security equipment -- it was designed not to kill anything. At worst, it would deliver an electric shock or spray an irritant -- enough to send any pesky creature on its way in short order.

Following the sound, George began to see signs of life on his monitors. At first, he only spotted a few winged insects, some of which ended up squashed on the windshield. As they drove further, he got more feedback from the sensors that indicated larger creatures in the distance.

While the trees looked shorter, the forest became denser the further they went from the LV1 and the beach. The tall trees cut off the light from above. In places where the palm fronds did not entirely blanket the sky, long shafts of light traveled at steep angles to the forest floor below. The EB5 sensors had no problem with the limited visibility. The light from their vehicle and the sunlight above attracted swarms of flying insects. George could see an occasional small furry mammal jump into the air, trying to catch them. It was hard for him to fathom that one day the dinosaurs would die and those small furry mammals would rule the earth.

Suddenly, a red light flashed on the dashboard. Vince said, "We have a *load*."

"Load? What does that mean?" asked George.

"L-O-D. Did you study any of the abbreviations? The Large Object Detector is picking up something on the other side of those trees." Vince pointed at the monitor for the hood mounted camera. George could not see anything on that screen except trees and bugs. On another monitor, he saw the yellow dot in the middle which represented the EB5. Directly ahead of them, he saw a red dot at least twice their size.

"I need a better view," said George.

Vince grabbed George's seatbelt so he could not unfasten it. "You are not getting out again," said the Chief of Security.

"Not out the door anyway," replied George. Then he grabbed a second seatbelt which made an X across his chest once secured. He hit a button on his armrest and a joystick popped out of the side right by his hand. "I paid some attention during training."

George pushed another button on his armrest and the roof of the EB5 slid open like an oversized sunroof. George's seat began to rise into the air on a large extension pole as thick as a modern telephone pole. The telescoping seat carried George thirty feet into the air.

"You're letting in bugs," called Vince.

George smiled at that. Without any extra lights on his rig, the bugs did not bother him. From his new vantage point, above the shorter treetops, he had a much better view of the forest. In the distance, George could see a lot of dust and debris being kicked up by some unseen force. He could also hear the sound of cracking and snapping trees. He had no guess what could be causing such destruction. Had he been in his own time he would have said it was a herd of bulldozers. Maybe he could not tell what it was, but he could tell where it was going. The EB5 sat directly in its path and it was coming quickly.

George lowered his seat as fast as the hydraulics would allow. The steel roof slid closed, but not before a hummingbird-sized dragonfly could escape. He looked at the *LOD* to see the giant red dot separating into a group of smaller red dots. He did not feel better about this because the new dots still looked bigger than the EB5.

"Uh, we've got company," said George.

Vince slammed the EB5 into reverse. At the same time, he hit a button marked *stealth*.

George continued, "We need to get off the trail."

Vince agreed. He smashed the EB5 through a thick patch of ferns and shut off the engine. George hoped the stealth mode would help. He knew a special alloy covered the outside body of the vehicle. It acted like an HDTV that could project any image captured by the EB5's cameras. They could essentially blend in with any surrounding like an octopus. An animal would have to crash into them to even know they were there.

George and Vince sat in silence as the ground outside started to rumble. The EB5 did its best to record every movement. The *LOD* started beeping louder as each proximity line was crossed. Vince turned off the audible alert. George agreed that silence was a good idea. He thought maybe they should make a run for it, but then the creatures were on top of them. George watched the video monitor, but all he could see was legs and tails. They seemed to be thundering by on four legs and they were in a hurry. For some reason they even broke off the trail and pounded their way through the ferns, rocking the EB5 on its suspension. The superior insulation of their vehicle could not keep out the tremendous sound of the stampede. George slapped his hands over his ears.

One of the last dinos in the herd collided with the EB5. It hit the back corner of the vehicle hard enough to slide it across the damp earth the way a spoiled child might kick a toy car across the kitchen tile.

The EB5 spun wildly and came to rest in the middle of the game trail. The control console went completely black leaving George and Vince in near darkness. Slowly, the on-board systems began to reboot and the interior lighting returned. A single warning light flashed near the steering column. Vince tapped a button to dismiss it.

George's heart pounded with his first real dinosaur encounter. A little shaken up, he patted his chest and thighs to make sure all of his body parts were still attached. If the experience bothered Vince, he hid it well. George assumed his military training helped him stay calm.

When the video cameras came back online, George looked for the herd. The dinos left a path of destruction, but no clue as to their species. The once thick, lush forest now looked like someone ran through there with the world's biggest lawn mower. Hundred year old trees had been snapped like saplings. George had to know more.

"Let's follow them," he said to Vince.

Switching off the stealth mode, Vince fired up the engine. The vehicle's safety system showed all clear, so Vince put it in gear. They went in search of the mysterious creatures.

CHAPTER THREE

"Breach attempt," announced the computer again.

First they lost the LV1's exterior cameras. Then they lost the downlink to the EB5. Parker worried what might go wrong next. Without the video surveillance, she could not see outside. Vince closed the steel shutters over the windows before he left with George. Only he had the authorization code to take the LV1 out of secure mode.

"Oh man, when is that thing going to stop?" asked Lloyd.

Parker looked at the security readout again. She had no idea what was happening outside. Her best guess was that something found them and was trying to get inside. She figured it had to be small because they could not feel any impact vibrations. The one good thing about being in secure mode, she thought, was the electro-net.

She explained to Lloyd, "The computer is letting us know something out there wants to get in here. I think the electro-net is keeping it back."

"You mean we are shocking some animal?" asked Sonya. "That sounds cruel."

Parker pointed at another monitor. It showed the output of the electro-net. She said, "It is very low voltage. Not enough to hurt anything, only scare it. It's the most humane way we could think of the keep the LV1 safe and us alive." She absently twirled a strand of her currently blue-tipped hair. "If only we could get the EB5 back online. I hope they're okay."

George noticed a flashing yellow light. He started to reach for it and Vince smacked his hand away.

"Don't touch anything if you don't know what it does," Vince snipped.

"How about a *please*," retorted George.

"Please." To George it sounded like more like a threat than a request. He liked Vince, but he was not sure the soldier liked him. Vince never seemed to relax. Maybe, thought George, he could win him over. If they were going to be constantly sharing the close quarters of the EB5, they would have to be friends.

George kept his hands to himself when he asked, "What does that flashing light mean?"

"Oh man," exclaimed Vince. "That's the uplink to the LV1. I bet we've been offline since that dino hit us."

Vince tapped the button directly below the warning light. George noticed the readout change on the middle of the five dashboard monitors. It read *uplink confirmed*.

Parker's voice came to them through the EB5's stereo speakers. She said, "There you are. You had us worried."

"You won't believe..." started George.

Vince interrupted, "Systems nominal. Initial contact with indigenous species. Nothing else to report."

Nothing else to report? George could not believe what Vince said. He announced, "We saw a living dinosaur. We saw a whole heard. We're following their trail now. I'm hoping to identify the species."

"Please be careful, George," said Parker.

She told *me* to be careful, thought George. He noticed she did not say it to Vince. Maybe that meant George's chances with her were better than he thought.

"Nothing else to report on this end," Parker finished.

The line went silent. George turned his attention back to the monitors. He looked at the damage caused by the heard, but could not stop smiling.

"What are you grinning at, lover boy?" asked Vince.

"Excited to see some dinos. That's all," said George.

"That's all." Vince did not sound convinced.

On the screen, George saw trees split and twisted. What species could be strong enough to cause such destruction? He once saw the aftermath of a North Texas tornado that was not even this destructive.

Through the narrow slit of the front windshield, George watched the forest turn into a dust cloud. Dark shapes moved inside the cloud. Looking down at the thermal imaging monitor on the dashboard, George hoped to get an idea of the size and shape of his quarry. A surprisingly clear image took shape.

Sauropods!

"I knew it!" he muttered. As they stampeded past him, he only caught a glimpse of thick legs and long tails. Somehow, he had a feeling what they might be. The image on the screen confirmed his belief with the outline of an enormous long-necked dinosaur. The different parts of the body appeared in different colors on the screen. The higher internal temperatures showed as red and turned to blue as they got colder. The stomach area of the Sauropod looked deep, dark red. It had to be putting off a tremendous amount of heat. The legs looked red, but not quite as dark. He guessed this had to do with the amount of muscle movement carrying such an enormous body. George knew that the more a muscle flexed and moved, the more heat it generated. The tail and neck looked a grey color and the head was a light blue that appeared almost white. The stomach must have been hot because decomposing plant material gives off heat. As the plants decomposed they acted like a huge furnace to keep the dinosaur warm. In the hottest part of the summer, he suspected the mighty beasts would have a very difficult time staying cool.

George thought that if the Sauropods saw the EB5 out in the open, they might panic and stampede. Or worse, they might feel threatened and try to crush the vehicle with him and Vince inside it. The close call they had with the herd earlier in the forest made George a little leery about getting too close.

Without a word, Vince knew to engage stealth mode. George wished he could see the outside of the EB5 as the cameras processed their environment and camouflaged the vehicle to match. Then Vince slowly eased toward the herd. He barely had his foot on the throttle. The EB5 continued to record everything around them.

Below one of the monitors, George found a wireless controller. George practiced with this one a lot. It reminded him of playing a video game. Mounted on top of the EB5, directly behind the sunroof, sat a thirty megapixel camera with both an optical and digital zoom. As the dust cleared, George trained in on the closest Sauropod. The powerful zoom lens allowed him to see the smallest details of the creature. The skin appeared to be very thick, colored like a modern elephant, but with very faint yellow patterns similar to those of a giraffe. Going up the neck, the grey seemed to turn light blue with a long black strip that went from the bottom of the neck all the way to the tip of the nose. The skin on its head was a much darker blue.

The other members of the herd appeared to be colored the same way, except for the biggest one. Its colors were much darker and, unlike the others, it had a very dark red coloration on its throat. George felt this one must be the Alpha leader of the pack. He wanted, rather, needed to figure out what species stood before him. He clicked the trigger button on the controller and heard the simulated sound of a camera shutter. His video camera took a still photo and the computer did the rest. The image on the screen started showing words down the left side:

LOCATION - ASIA
TIME PERIOD - LATE CRETACEOUS
ENVIRONMENT - PALM AND CYCAD FOREST
DINOSAURIA ORDER/SUBORDER - SAUROPOD
ESTIMATED SIZE - 30 TO 50 FEET LONG.

After that, red outlines of every possible Sauropod began flashing on the screen. They went by faster than George could identify them. Luckily, he did not have to. The computer did all the work. In less than thirty seconds, it found a match and announced it with big green letters covering the entire screen. George tapped the touchscreen and the word **MATCH** disappeared. He could now see the red outline following the exact shape of the dinosaur. Now on the left, at the bottom of the list of information, it read:

NAME - NEMEGTOSAURUS

George knew this species. His uncle taught him a lot growing up. Because of that, he knew by the end of the Jurassic Period nearly all members of the Sauropod family had become extinct. A few species managed to survive all the way to the end of the late Cretaceous Period when they, along with all other non-avian dinosaurs, became extinct. The majority of the long necks that survived into late Cretaceous were from the Titanosaurus family. Although not as large as their earlier cousins, they were still massive dinosaurs and among the largest living things on earth by the end of the Cretaceous Period.

George resumed his video and turned the camera toward another Nemegtosaurus feeding on the top of a tree. He could see that these dinosaurs did not actually chew their food. They appeared to use their peg-like teeth to rake the leaves off of the limbs. Then they swallowed the leaves whole without chewing. He guessed they must use gastroliths to grind their food, like some modern reptiles and birds. Gastroliths are small stones that the animal would swallow and hold in its stomach. As the stomach churns and moves, it causes these stones to rub against each other and crush up the plant material—the way teeth would do if the plants were chewed. Like most other members of the Sauropod family, the jaw muscles and tooth design of Nemegtosaurus appeared to be very weak, making it difficult to actually chew their food. This, along with the amount of time it took to chew every bite, made it more efficient for the dinosaur to use gastroliths to help grind their food rather than use their jaws and teeth.

From memory, George recalled that Nemegtosaurus lived at a time when most predators were much too small to be a threat to an adult of its species. However, the babies were always in mortal danger from a variety of different predators. To insure their safety, the adults would keep the juveniles secure by keeping them in the center of the herd. Surrounded by the adults, practically no contemporary predator would dare attempt an attack on the juveniles.

George wanted to get a closer look at the huge herbivores in person. He silently gestured for Vince to drive closer. Vince agreed, but stopped about one hundred feet from the main herd. George hurriedly strapped in to activate his telescoping seat. The sunroof slid silently open and George lifted up past the rooftop camera and on up into the air. He immediately noticed the overpowering odor from the dinosaurs. They must produce a tremendous amount of digestive gas, he suspected.

Now at the same height with the adult Nemegtosaurs, he could see them clearly. They had to be able to see him, but appeared unconcerned by his presence. George imagined they regarded him as a stray Sauropod of some kind – he was the head on top of a long metal neck. They did not seem panicked or the least bit worried about him being there.

George noticed a female using her front legs to push on a tree. She leaned into the tree with all of her massive weight and it cracked under the strain. Earlier, when George heard the sound of trees snapping, he assumed it was because the Sauropods were making room to walk in the forest. Now, he knew that was not the reason for them knocking down the trees. This one had a more maternal reason. Once the female knocked the tree down, the adorable babies rushed in and began to eat the leaves. George laughed at their surprising speed. He realized that the babies were too short to reach the more tender leaves that grew in the very tops of the trees. Since they could not reach, mom was bringing the treetops down to their level. This behavior suggested that these dinosaurs were better parents than what early paleontologists may have thought.

The herd continued to graze and push their way deeper into the forest. George saw no sign of what might have caused their stampede. He watched the interaction with the juveniles and did not realize that something was standing directly behind him—staring intently. At first, George smelled something awful. It smelled similar to the distant herd only much stronger. Then he felt hot breath on the back of his head and neck. He slowly rotated his chair to see what was behind him. There, only four feet away, a huge Nemegtosaurus leaned toward him. Its crimson head suggested that it was a male. It stood as tall as George in his elevated seat. George's *Charm* bracelet beeped twice and Vince's voice came to him through the wrist-radio.

"George, we have a *LOD* directly behind us."

George wanted to tell Vince that he was well aware of their situation. However, he decided it would be better to remain still. One wrong move and this creature would crush him, Vince and the EB5. George quietly stared into the bulbous black eyes of the Nemegtosaurus.

When George was a kid, Uncle Evert taught him that if you look at an animal directly in the eyes, it is usually considered a threat. Remembering this, George lowered his head in a submissive gesture and hoped the Sauropod would simply walk away. Apparently, the Nemegtosaurus had no intention of moving. It leaned a little closer and inhaled, trying to recognize the scent of this strange animal that sat paralyzed before it. George noticed that the Sauropod did not act scared or startled. If anything, it seemed confused. It must have thought George, and by extension, the EB5 combined to make a new type of Sauropod. Maybe it thought the man and vehicle was a long lost member of the herd.

George could never know how right he was. Although the Nemegtosaurus was enormous, it had a brain no larger than a common chicken egg. That small brain did not have a lot of room for anything too complicated. It probably interpreted its environment by instinct. It understood basic things like food and danger. It had no way of comprehending this boy from the future and his amazing machine.

It came closer to sniff again. George wanted to reach out and touch it. He really wanted to feel the texture of its skin. From his up-close vantage point, he could tell the skin was neither scaly like a lizard, nor textured like an elephant's. The best way he could think to describe it was to compare it to the legs of a tortoise. George took a chance and slowly reached his hand out to touch the Nemegtosaurus. Apparently, Sauropods do not show a lot of emotion toward one another or touch each other's heads. The giant dinosaur abruptly pulled his head back out of reach. At that point, George decided it might be a good idea to get out of this situation before something bad happened.

George put his hand on the armrest joystick and lowered himself back down into the EB5. As he came down, the Nemegtosaurus lowered its head at the same rate. What was it thinking, George wanted to know. Did it think he was playing with it? Throughout history, George remembered that animals have always used different movements or actions to convey certain messages to one another. George could not predict that in *Nemegtosaurus language* when one male lowers its head in the presence of another, it is a clear sign that it wants to fight. As far as the Nemegtosaurus was concerned, the strange looking creature in front of him was displaying all the signs of a challenge.

The Nemegtosaurus took a deep breath and roared loudly. The sound forced George to cover his ears. It reminded him when his older brother took him to the railroad tracks as a child. They would stand at a safe distance and listen to the diesel engines thunder past; rumbling and clacking. He could feel the sound vibrating through his body now, the same as he did then.

The male Nemegtosaurus leaned back and stood upright on its hind legs increasing his height by nearly twenty feet. The Sauropod towered over them. As George continued to lower himself into the EB5, he looked down at Vince. The hardened soldier's eyes looked as big as his face. If George felt scared, then Vince looked twice as terrified. The Nemegtosaurus pawed at the air with his front legs as the armored sunroof slid closed. It unleashed another massive roar, but the EB5 dampened the sound.

Before Vince could drive, the Nemegtosaurus dropped to all fours. George thought he felt the EB5 do a little hop from the shockwave. The Sauropod did not attack. Maybe, George deduced, it could not understand what happened to the stranger. If another Sauropod no longer challenged the Alpha, then it had no reason to fight. They watched on the monitor as the mighty creature moved back to the tree line and resumed eating.

"We should go," suggested George.

"Good idea," replied Vince. He did not look quite as serious and seemed a little more open to George's suggestions.

George thought being that close to the Nemegtosaurus was very exciting. However, the sheer size and power of the dinosaur was something to keep in mind. It would not be good to be caught in the middle of another stampede. George wanted to start looking for signs of his uncle. He knew they now had less than twenty-four hours and time was running out. Besides, they were likely to encounter some other species. Vince turned off the stealth and engaged a homing beacon that would lead them to the LV1. George loosened his extra safety harness as Vince drove them back toward the beach.

CHAPTER FOUR

Keep it together, Sonya told herself. *It's out there and I'm safe in here.* In truth, Sonya worried less about whatever animal caused the breach alert than the bacteria it could bring into the sterile environment of the LV1. The computer announced the breach attempt twelve times already. It started to ring like clockwork. Parker still could not get the cameras working – and no way would Sonya allow Lloyd to open the door.

"I can't wait for George and Vince to come back," she whispered.

As long as the uplink stayed connected, Vince had no problem following the beacon. Of course, the dino herd left a nice wide path for them to follow.

Watching the swaying palm leaves, George wished he could feel the warm breeze as they zoomed along through the forest. It may be more humid than Florida, but the moving air would be a relief from the close confines of the EB5. Dr. Morgan and his team of scientists packed so much into the super-charged SUV that they barely had room for the two passengers.

Instead of watching out the steel-plated window, George watched the monitors for any new encounters. The LOD would alert him to anything large, but the smaller creatures would go unnoticed at their current speed.

George decided to call the roof mounted camera the All Knowing Eye. He knew the EB5 would record everything around them, but all that video would have to be reviewed by technicians once they went back through the Goal. He spun the Eye back and forth watching for anything exciting. He spotted a small stream that snaked through the forest. Either they were not following the same trail back or they somehow missed this earlier.

"Slow down," George pleaded.

Vince did and looked at the Eye monitor. George focused on a group of long-snouted crocodilians lying on the bank with their jaws wide open. A flock of small birds walked carelessly in and out of their gaping jaws as they picked the crocodilians teeth clean. *George* chuckled. He thought of them as the world's first dentists. Vince stopped the vehicle so its sensors could take in all the new data. The crocodilians, now aware of their presence, slipped one by one into the dark water and out of sight. Much like modern crocodiles, these early ancestors fled to the safety of the water not only to hide, but to prepare to catch anything that came down to drink.

With nothing else to see, Vince resumed driving down the trail. They started to spot a lot of small reptiles and mammals scurrying across the forest floor in the afternoon warmth. The creatures dodged in and out of the fern bushes that dotted the area. One animal, in particular, really caught George's attention. A lizard, approximately four inches long, raced across the trail in front of the EB5. It climbed halfway up the tree and then leaped into the air. As it left the tree, a large flap of skin attached to its front legs opened on each side of the lizard and it glided through the air. Using its tail as a rudder, and leaning its body to one side, the lizard banked like a fighter jet and landed on the trunk of another tree nearly twenty yards away.

"Did you see that!" exclaimed George. "That little dude is an awesome flyer!"

George instinctively pulled at his door handle. He wanted to get out for a closer look, but Vince had the auto-lock engaged. Maybe the Nemegtosaurus did not teach me a lesson, George thought. The lizard leaped to the next tree, again sailing an amazing distance. Before the EB5 passed the flying lizard, a creature, about the size of an owl, suddenly swooped down from its perch above and grabbed the lizard in midair. At first, *George* thought it must have been some sort of bird, but when it landed on the ground it quickly ran into the woods on only its back legs. It was no bird. It was a flying dinosaur!

George hoped the Eye would identify the new predator. He watched it scan, but find no match. Whatever it was, for now, would remain a mystery. Vince did not slow down for a second look. The soldier concentrated on his driving. George looked at the topographic map. It appeared that they were angling steadily away from the LV1, while still heading toward the beach.

"Do you know where you're going?" asked George.

"We're supposed to be looking for Professor Stone," replied Vince. "Did you see that island when we first got here? If we come around from the south, that will give us the shortest distance, shore to shore."

Why did Vince care about the island, George wondered. Did he have some secret information?

Vince continued, "While you've been bouncing up and down in your lift chair playing dinosaur hunter, I was studying the map. Zoom in on the southern tip of the island and you will see a fading heat signature."

George did. It looked like a near perfect circle. Now almost black, whatever heat it had must be fading quickly.

"What is it?" asked George.

"I only say this because I am an expert survivalist, but it looks like a campfire."

George's heart pounded. Could it be his uncle? Could he be trapped on that island? "Let's go!" shouted George.

They plowed ahead through the forest as the vegetation grew thicker and darker. The video cameras became mostly worthless in the mid-day darkness. Vince would not allow George to turn on the spotlights. He drove by infrared, swerving around yellow and light blue trees as they appeared on the screen. Then Vince slammed on the brakes. An enormous red heat signature, about the size of an Army tank blocked their path. It sat low to the ground and appeared to have a very rough body texture. George guessed it to be some kind of Ankylosaur. He turned the Eye in the direction of the creature for confirmation. The video camera peered into the darkness. Soon, an outline of the image appeared. It cycled through a bunch of possibilities. The thing seemed to have a large number of small heat sources on its back and sides. What could cause those heat spikes, wondered George. Could it be injured? Maybe it had holes in its armor where body heat escaped.

Finally, Vince hit the switch for the exterior flood lights. At the same time, the Eye responded with the species identification. Saichania. George studied many different types of Ankylosaurs. He knew the Saichania to average about twenty-three feet in length. Thick boney armor covered most of its body, including its skull, neck and stomach. Like its North American cousins, it had a heavy club at the end of its tail for defense.

The Saichania squinted at their bright lights. George assumed it must have weak eyesight and preferred the dark of the forest. With the light, George could now see what caused the red flares on the thermal imaging. A small flock of Pterosaurs perched on the larger dino's back. He remembered that modern rhinoceroses and the Red-Billed Oxpecker birds from Africa have a similar relationship. By riding on the back of the rhino, the birds remain safe from attackers. In return for their safety, they pick the parasites off of the rhino and also act as lookouts for danger. The Oxpeckers have much better eyesight than the rhino. These Pterosaurs must have the same symbiotic relationship with the Saichania. They have protection while riding on a Saichania's back. In return they warn the dinosaur of approaching danger.

Now, the Pterosaurs started to circle over the Saichania, squawking shrilly. The massive Ankylosaur began to sniff the air, trying to get a fix on the intruder. George knew it could not smell them sealed inside the EB5. But, as with all animals, if one of its senses is limited another sense usually compensates for it. In the case of Saichania, its eyesight seemed to be poor but its hearing and sense of smell had to be unequalled in the dinosaur kingdom. If it moved downwind from the EB5, it would surely smell the environmentally-friendly exhaust. Then the creature would know exactly where they were. Like the LV1, the EB5 had a hydrogen engine. While the exhaust fumes were not toxic like a combustion engine, it did have a unique odor.

The Pterosaurs, however, apparently had excellent eyesight. They flew directly at the EB5 and started circling the lights. They screeched and squawked as loud as they could. Either they were trying to scare off the stranger or they wanted to attract the attention of the Saichania. George looked at Vince. He already shifted into reverse and floored the pedal. The spinning wheels shredded the ferns and kicked mud into the air. George assumed the Ankylosaur would not follow. It was not a natural predator and should not chase them.

George assumed wrong.

The Saichania bellowed like a six-ton bull. It lunged forward at an amazing speed for such a huge animal. The five hundred horsepower engine should have easily outrun the charging animal. Except, Vince backed directly into a tree. Before he could re-route, the Saichania came up alongside them. This close, the lights must have hurt its eyes. It probably did not like the smell of the engine either, thought George. It immediately turned sideways and smashed the EB5 with its massive tail club. Inside the vehicle, George would have been thrown into Vince's lap if not for his seatbelt.

Before they could recover, the Saichania slammed the EB5 again. This time the rear of the vehicle lifted, momentarily, off the ground.

"Turn off the lights," ordered George.

Vince flipped the switch, but that did not keep the Saichania from striking them a third time. This one knocked the EB5 sideways. The tires slid across the muddy ground, pinning Vince's door against another tree.

Parker's voice came over George's *Charm*. "I'm getting some weird readings. What's going on George?"

"I, uh, can't really talk right now," he said, automatically holding his wrist up to his mouth. He forgot that she told him he did not have to have the microphone so close.

"Too loud," Parker said. He thought he heard a slight chuckle. Great, he thought, at least she is amused.

George did not know how many hits the EB5 could take. He wondered how bad the stainless steel armor had been dented so far. Then he had another thought about their fully-equipped vehicle. He grabbed the *Eye* controller and said to Vince, "Hit the stealth mode when I have the dino in my sights."

George pointed the *Eye* directly at the Saichania. He had no idea if it would work, but he hoped the EB5 would capture the image of the rampaging Ankylosaur and project it on the outside of their vehicle. If it did not work, the dinosaur would likely crush them like an aluminum soda can.

When Vince activated the stealth, the Saichania suddenly stopped. It must be working. George would love to see what the EB5 looked like at this moment. The near-sighted dino probably thought another of its species wondered into the woods. The Ankylosaur's pause gave George another opportunity. He reached in front of Vince and pushed hard on the EB5's horn. The blast startled everybody outside and inside the EB5. The Pterosaurs disappeared up into the trees. The Saichania stumbled backward a few steps.

Vince took the opportunity to move. He slammed the accelerator and peeled out of their dead end. Watching the infrared, George thought for a moment that the Saichania would give chase. It seemed quite aggressive for an herbivore.

Back on track for the beach, George had one other thought. Maybe the Saichania saw the EB5 as a potential mate. Although it was a little smaller, the EB5 had the right shape, especially if the stealth mode projected the image of another Ankylosaur. So far, he and Vince encountered two large dino species and they had two harrowing experiences. It seemed like they kept heading straight into danger. Thankfully, Dr. Morgan's technology and equipment kept them safe. He wondered how his uncle would handle it without any of the special tools.

"Are you guys alright?" asked Parker over the EB5 communicator.

"Yeah," answered George. "We made a new friend."

"That's nice," she replied. She did not sound very thrilled. "I wanted to let you know we are having a few technical difficulties here. Nothing major. Also, the countdown clock says we have twenty hours until recall."

Recall meant when the LV1 would automatically return through the *Goal*. George knew that he, Vince and the EB5 had to be back inside the LV1 before that clock hit zero. He could not believe they had already been here for four hours. He had several unbelievable experiences in such few short hours. With things happening so fast, George had no idea how they would find his uncle in time.

CHAPTER FIVE

"Twenty-two is my lucky number, man," announced Lloyd. He watched the breach alert as it continued to count higher. Without the exterior cameras, they could not see what wanted to get into the LV1. Lloyd did not personally work on the electro-net, but he knew the guy that designed it. The low voltage warning system should scare away most animals and people.

Lloyd thought aloud, "Like, do you think it's an Amazonian or something?" He imagined seven foot tall women standing outside, trying to open the LV1.

"First of all, Amazonians come from the Amazon. Not Asia," said Parker. "Secondly, um, oh yeah. They're not real."

Sonya added, "If I understand correctly, there were no humans alive during this era."

Lloyd looked at the two women.

"Harsh, man. Harsh," said Lloyd. Being the oldest member of the team, Lloyd experienced a lot in his life. Time Travel and dinosaurs seemed far out to him, but nothing to be unmellow about. However, he would totally lose his cool if some of the characters from his favorite comic books came for a visit. Until then, he would keep the vehicles running and keep counting the breach attempts.

George wanted an excuse to talk to Parker. He really started to like her and wanted to hear the sound of her voice. He pushed the talk button on his *Charm*.

"Hey Parker, we're going to check out that island."

He liked the musical quality of her voice, even when she spoke matter-of-fact. "What island?"

Vince interjected, "You should be able to see it on video. Look at the rear display."

"Oh," answered Parker. "That's one of our minor technical difficulties. We have no external video or sensors and you locked the security shutters."

Vince looked sternly at George. George could tell he was aggravated. The former Marine said, "The island will have to wait. We're coming back to the LV1. You guys can't be sitting blind."

George had mixed feelings. The route back to the LV1 would use valuable time that he could be searching for Professor Stone. On the other hand, it would be good to get out of the EB5 and stretch his legs. Not to mention, visit with Parker.

On the beach, it felt to George like the EB5 moved slower. Maybe not having the trees whizzing by on either side changed his perspective. Then again, maybe the wheels had a harder time finding traction on the sand. Up ahead, he could see the back of the LV1 sticking out of the trees.

Vince stopped short. The body of what looked like one of those little flying dinosaurs they saw back in the woods blocked the path. Vince unbuckled his seatbelt.

"Stay here," he ordered.

"Wait, are you getting out?" asked George. It did not seem fair that Vince could leave the EB5 and he could not. After their previous encounters, George was not sure if he really did want to get out. He did not like being treated like a little kid though.

"That *thing* is blocking the way. If it's hurt, I'm not going to run over it," said Vince.

George thought that made sense. Vince climbed out and closed his door. George listened to it hiss as it sealed. Then he grabbed the *Eye* control to watch Vince. He kept his watch on the other monitors to make sure nothing came up behind them.

Luckily, Vince wore his leather driving gloves. The animal dripped blood when he picked it up. George could tell it was already dead. He zoomed in with the camera to see a single slash across the little dino's belly. Then George turned the camera toward the LV1. A flash of light caught his attention. Once the camera focused, however, he could not see anything unusual. He remembered something about an electric field that worked like a shield to protect the vehicle from intruders. He wondered if it would flash or spark when something got too close.

Panning back toward Vince, he saw the soldier toss the body into the bushes at the edge of the sand. He started back toward the EB5. Long after the plants should have stopped moving from Vince's throw, George saw a fern shake. He knew something was hiding there. George switched the center monitor to show what the right side cameras recorded. At first, it looked like a normal forest.

Then he saw them.

It reminded him of the hidden picture game in the magazine at the doctor's office. The hidden objects were not easy to see with one glance. As he stared at the image, George suddenly started seeing several pairs of eyes staring back at him. Before things went crazy, he counted a dozen pair. Suddenly, everything seemed clear.

The staring eyes belonged to Velociraptors. Their ambush worked perfectly. George's uncle once theorized that raptors hunting in packs would use dead animals as bait. They would use the small animal to lure a larger animal into their trap. The bigger scavenger would instantly become prey to the surprise attack of a dozen or more raptors. This time, Vince was the prey.

George had no way to warn Vince. Before he could even hit the horn, the raptors sprang from cover. They came silently, not even an attack bellow. They did not screech like they did in Hollywood movies. Silence and surprise proved to be their best weapons. Professor Stone used to theorize that pre-historic humans had a sixth sense – that strange feeling someone is staring at us or is trying to sneak up behind us. It is a built-in sense that helped them survive. He said it has been passed down through the generations, but technology has dulled that sense. George's uncle believed that people now rely more on computers to tell them about their environment than their own instincts. The first humans had a much harder life and were subjected to many more dangers than our lives today. Still, modern humans can tell when their life is in danger. Vince seemed to have a strong sixth sense. Almost as fast as the raptors sprang their trap, Vince looked over his shoulder.

The raptors cut off Vince's return to the EB5. He ducked as one of them pounced. It sailed over his head. The ferocious creature rolled in the sand and rapidly bounced back up on both legs. It raised its deadly claws for another attack. Vince faced a wall of raptors between him and the EB5. Some of the predators started to circle behind him. George thought if it had been only one or two that Vince could have easily defended himself. George had no way to help. With a dozen raptors outside, neither of them stood a chance.

Then Vince did something unexpected. He raced toward the surf as the raptor pack converged on him. Leaping into the air, he straightened his body and dove headfirst into the waves. The raptors never slowed. They rushed headlong into the surf, following him. This astonished George. He never would have thought to escape that way. George hoped the pack would not follow Vince out into the water, but he was sadly mistaken. These raptors could swim, and they were not about to give up on their dinner. As Vince swam into deeper water, the raptors followed. They swung their arms madly, as they swiped and clawed in his direction. They fought against the small waves and kept getting closer. George zoomed in with the *Eye* to see the raptors' jaws snapping open and closed, chugging water and gasping for air. Vince continued to swim further from shore. George checked the topographical map. He guessed Vince was getting close to the point where the sea bed dropped sharply. Soon he would be in deep water.

The waves kept George from having a clear view of the nerve-wracking action. He switched the *Eye* to thermal and could clearly see the red bodies as if they were now floating in mid-air. A large red shape swam behind and below Vince, then it was gone. George now worried that if the raptors did not get Vince, something else would. He wanted to do something to help. George started repeatedly honking the horn. He watched the *Eye* monitor. The sound caught the attention of some of the raptors in the rear. This slowed the pack long enough for Vince to react. The soldier dove down deep. He swam under the raptors. From the thermal image, it looked like their killing claws barely missed him as they treaded water. Vince raced for the shore.

The sudden change in direction caused the lead raptors to stop their advance. The middle of the pack piled on those in front like a car wreck on an overcrowded freeway. The extra weight caused them to push each other under the surface. Maybe, George hoped, that would thin their numbers. They seemed to be in an all-out brawl for survival. Their prey momentarily forgotten. Only a few stragglers managed to get back on Vince's trail. He emerged to refill his lungs with a much needed breath. The slowest raptors were now the ones closest to him.

Once Vince reached the shore, he scrambled through the sand toward EB5. A pair of raptors nipped at his heels. George had an idea. He climbed behind the steering wheel to his right. Then he opened the left side passenger door. Vince practically dove into George's now unoccupied seat. This dive did not look quite as graceful as the one heading into the water, thought George.

"Go! Go! Go!" ordered Vince.

George stomped his foot on the pedal. The EB5 peeled away even before Vince had his door closed. Checking the rear view in the monitor, George saw the raptors regroup before giving chase. There seemed to be one in charge. It, probably a male, had a red stripe down the back of its yellowish head and only one eye. The others looked to him before taking action. George concentrated on his driving. He closed the distance between them and the LV1 as fast as possible. At the last second, he tapped a button on his

Charm and the back hatch lowered for them to drive safely inside. The raptors lagged too far behind to catch them before the LV1 door closed.

When they climbed out of the EB5, Sonya said to Vince, "You're soaking. What happened?"

Parker said, "Don't tell me you made some more new friends."

"I wouldn't call these guys friendly," said George. "A pack of Velociraptors ambushed us."

"Maybe those are the same things that have been hitting us all day." Parker took George over to the monitor and showed him the log displaying twenty-two breach attempts. It amazed George that they tried more than once with the electro-net activated.

George thought about this for a moment. He thought that it showed intelligence and cunning. He knew paleontologists suspected members of the raptor family to be smarter than most other dinosaurs. What he witnessed moments ago seemed way more advanced than anyone could have expected. He assumed the repeated breach attempts meant they were attacking in different spots. Could they have memory, wondered George. Could they attack one spot, remember that and then choose a different spot to test for weakness? Or maybe, he countered, they were so dumb that they kept attacking over and over, getting shocked each time and not expecting it to happen again. He wished Parker had some video surveillance to show him. It appeared the cameras were still down.

Vince appeared next to them with a towel draped around his neck. He said, "First priority, get those cameras back online. We are not going outside again until we are sure those little nasties are gone."

George disagreed with Vince. They needed to get back out there as soon as possible. They needed to get over to that island. If his uncle was over there, he could need their help. He might be hurt. Knowing that the raptors could swim did not make George feel any better. They could be heading to the island right now for all he knew. Vince barely survived the raptor attack. George did not want to think what might happen to Professor Stone.

CHAPTER SIX

George snapped awake. For a second he believed he was back in Florida with his uncle. The day at the mammoth dig site felt like so long ago. His mind tricked him into thinking that the time-traveling experiment was the dream. It only seemed possible to see real, living dinosaurs in movies or dreams. Looking around the cockpit of the LV1, everything came back into focus. He wiped the sleep out of his eyes.

"How long was I out?" he asked.

"I don't know, man. Maybe two hours," offered Lloyd.

Two hours! How could they let him waste valuable time? George needed to be out looking for his uncle. He could not sit here taking a nap. He jumped up and went looking for Vince.

Before George could express his concern, Vince said, "You ready to get back out there?"

"Uh," was all George could manage. He half expected Vince to want to stay in the LV1 until it was time to go home.

Parker slung her arm around George's shoulders. He felt that increasingly familiar blush come to his cheeks. She said, "We got the cameras and external sensors working. You don't want to know how much code I had to re-write. I sent up the *Balloon* and got some pretty good readings of your island."

The *Balloon* was exactly that, a tethered balloon. It looked more like a miniature hot air balloon. Instead of having a basket for miniature people, it had a box of all sorts of equipment that George never even pretended to memorize. He knew it could tell the weather and take long range scans. The cable that connected it to the LV1 could extend up to one hundred feet. At that height, he knew the *Balloon's* readings could read farther than the EB5's on-board sonar.

Vince added, "There's a lot of activity over there. The thermal shows too many medium and small life signs. But we have a dozen other problems to worry about first. Look at this."

He pointed to the monitor showing the rear of the LV1. The raptor pack paced in the sand. None of them charged the LV1. George thought they must be learning.

"We have to get rid of those things before we can take the EB5 back out. We can't risk having the back hatch open that long," explained Vince.

That meant guns. George did not particularly like weapons of any kind. At least the ones that Dr. Morgan designed were non-lethal. They would not be killing any dinos. Hopefully the guns would scare away the raptors. Vince already had the weapon cabinet unlocked. They had two surge guns and a stun rod for each of them. The bulky surge gun with its backpack power supply would have to be strapped on and used at close range. George did not really want to go back outside, even with a gun.

"What about *Big Daddy*?" George asked. He thought if Vince wanted to use the surge guns, why not use the big one mounted on top of the LV1. If the smaller backpack guns could shoot concussive blasts of air at the individual raptors, then maybe *Big Daddy* could get them all at once.

"We would only have one shot," said Vince. "You know Big Daddy will take ten minutes to build up enough air pressure for another shot. If we miss, then we still have to go outside with the backpacks."

It seemed like it would be worth a try. Dr. Morgan told George that the smaller surge guns could knock the feathers off a chicken. Big Daddy supposedly could bring an elephant to its knees when it fired its directed blast of air. Even if they had to wait ten minutes between shots, that seemed better than the thirty second recharge time of the personal units. Thirty seconds did not seem like a long time. But when you are face-to-face with a hungry Velociraptor, it could mean the difference between life and death.

Vince sat at the *Big Daddy* control station. George watched the rear monitor while the rooftop gun charged. He noticed the raptors stayed mostly in the area about twenty feet behind the LV1. They stayed safely away from the electro-net. Some of them came and went, but only one never moved. George chose to call this one Lefty since he only had his left eye. The red striped Velociraptor surely lost his right eye in some forgotten battle or hunt. The fact that he survived with such an injury proved him worthy to be the Alpha of this pack. Lefty waited patiently.

Finally, Vince was ready to fire *Big Daddy*. He did not wait for a countdown or secret signal. He aimed and fired without ceremony. THWOOMP. George imagined it like throwing a basketball into a sand box, except there was no ball. The blast of air left a rounded crater in the sand a few inches deep. The displaced sand flew into the air along with six raptors. Lefty landed on his feet and scampered into the woods. Three of the raptors hit the ground unconscious. The other two knocked back from the shot wobbled out of sight. The rest of the pack bolted, most likely startled by the sound that accompanied the blast.

"Time to go, George," said Vince as he got up from his station.

"I think they'll be back," started George.

"Then let's not waste time finding out." Vince ushered him to the left side passenger door of the EB5.

"Where are we going?" asked George.

"You are going to the island," said Vince.

"No way is there room for two people in Princess Caroline. This is a one man operation," said Lloyd.

Vince made sure George was strapped into his seat. He practiced one day with the Princess Caroline mini-sub, but he did not know how he would get into it with it wedged in the back of the EB5. There did not seem to be enough room to climb around all of the other equipment. Maybe Vince was going to drive out by the water and help him unload.

"I had Lloyd put one of the surge guns in with your other supplies. You've got twelve hours, but I want a report every hour or I'm swimming out to get you," said Parker.

It seemed like she cared about him and that made George feel strangely warm. Then she leaned into the EB5, their heads almost touching. She reached past him and pushed a button on the console. George's chair spun around backwards, then tipped him face down. If he had not been strapped in, he would have fallen on the floor. The back end of Princess Caroline opened and the chair pushed him inside. He felt the seat snap in place and the remote arm retracted behind him. Once the sub-cycle hatch sealed, the control panel came to life.

He wished he could have seen his exit from outside of the LV1.

Lloyd lowered the rear ramp. From outside, the late afternoon glare would have made the opening look dark, almost black. George revved the engine and an instant later the bright yellow pod shot out of the back. The sub-cycle flew through the air a few feet before touching down in the sand. The perfectly balanced vehicle did not lose a second as it sped away from the LV1. George hesitated about leaving the command center until he had his hands on Princess Caroline's handlebars. The humming engine fueled his excitement. He completely forgot about the raptors as he raced toward the water.

The sub-cycle kept its pace as it hit the surf. George never thought he would use Princess Caroline, so he did not know exactly how to enter the water. Back at the lab, during training, they used a crane to lower him into the diving pool. Although the lapping water slowed his inertia, the sub-cycle kept going forward even when the water rose above his semi-circle viewing portal. When the cycle no longer touched the wet sand, the submarine functions activated. George could feel the change as he went from driving to floating. He looked around for any leaks. None. Good. Then he hoped his lack of knowledge in this craft would not come back to haunt him.

When George cleared the breakers, the ocean water became surprisingly clear. The waves caused so much churn that he could not see anything at first. Once he got past the unsettled sand, George could see plenty through the wide viewing portal. In about seven or eight feet of water, he spotted a large number of ammonites floating beneath him. They looked like squids that lived coiled inside spiral shells. During the day they pulled their soft bodies into their shells and slept. But at night, these attractive little creatures became voracious hunters, attacking and eating anything smaller than they were. George knew that some ammonites grew to very large sizes. Using their parrot like beaks to rip open prey, the largest ones were capable of killing something as large as a grown man. He was glad that he was safely inside the mini-sub and most of them were still asleep.

Sailing past the drop unsettled George. He could see the sandy bottom one moment and then nothing but deep blue water the next. The undersea cliff dropped off further than the sun could reach as it glinted through the surface from above. He checked the small dial that acted as both a compass and sonar. Nothing showed. Thinking about the large creature that swam past Vince earlier gave him goose bumps. From the LV1, he had to cross a greater distance than where Vince originally wanted to cross.

Thankfully the trip did not take too long. Princess Caroline rolled up onto a packed clay beach and George opened the hatch. If he felt crowded in the EB5, the sub-cycle made him feel claustrophobic. Down the beach, George saw the bloated remains of some unidentifiable sea creature washed up on shore. Several large Pterosaurs fed on the carcass.

Wanting to get a better look, George climbed out of the sub-cycle. He rolled it safely away from the water's edge and walked toward the dead creature. The smell of the decaying body rapidly became unbearable. However, his curiosity to identify the creature pushed him closer. George held his arm up to his nose in an effort to block the smell. Even that did very little to cover the terrible odor.

The creature looked about seven feet long. It had a long skinny snout filled with hundreds of small teeth. Two large flippers stuck out almost right behind the head. George thought it looked like a young Plesiosaurus. Something did not make sense to him. Where was the back half of this swimming reptile? Moving around behind the partial carcass answered his question. He could clearly see bite marks. Something bit the young Plesiosaur in half! What could have done this? The animal that bit this thing in half must have been huge!

Realizing that he had just crossed the very ocean where this giant predator may have been lurking, a cold chill went up George's neck. He hoped that he would not run into the creature on his trip back to the mainland. George walked over to the sub-cycle and pulled out the equipment from the side compartments. The surge gun took up most of the room on one side. Next to that, he found a metallic silver case about the size of a common briefcase. On the opposite side of the cycle, he removed the waterproof case's larger counterpart.

He moved up to the tree line and found a small clearing backed up to the sheer rocky hillside. It was not quite steep enough to be called a cliff, but it had enough slope that he thought nothing could sneak up on him. It seemed like a good place to make camp. George opened the smaller of the two silver cases. This one contained some nutrient packs and basic tools for making a fire and cooking (if he needed to hunt or fish). It also held a cloth satchel that he could sling over his shoulder to hold any artifacts he might find. It seemed reasonable that he could drop in a few nutrient packs when he went hiking away from camp.

The second case contained the *toys*. He reminded himself that he was on an island and Vince said there were no large predators. Still, better safe than dino chow. First, he removed six stands that looked like short camera tripods. Each one stood only twelve inches high. With his back to the rock wall, George would not have to make a complete circle. He started at one side of the hill and spaced out the stands in a big arc until he came back to the wall. He remembered from training that he did not have to line up the receivers exactly. As long as he did not space them too far apart, the portable electro-net would protect him from the ground up to about three feet. He knew raptors could jump, but if they did not see an obstacle they might walk directly into the electric field.

With the electro-net in place, George could now concentrate on setting up the other defensive weapon. This one also had a tripod, about three feet tall with a swivel head. The device that went on top of that swivel head impressed him. George removed the heavy object from its custom-cut foam space and mounted it. Lloyd called it the *Hammer of Thor*. George smiled at this. He knew Lloyd loved his comic books and mythological heroes.

The *Hammer* looked like a small Gatling-type cannon. It had six barrels grouped into a single rotating cylinder. Once positioned on the tripod, it could spin three hundred and sixty degrees and tilt as high as a seventy degree angle. If George remembered correctly, it could fire its plastic pellet ammo at ten thousand rounds per minute with a range of fifty yards. It had less than half the cool down time of a traditional combustion weapon. The only real limitation was the amount of ammunition he could carry. Although each pellet was roughly the size of a BB, he had to have someplace to put them.

This was truly an autocannon. It had a heat and motion sensor with a programmable perimeter. George could set it to the maximum range of fifty yards or lower the awareness to as little as ten yards. He did not like the idea of letting anything get that close. As he had seen with the Saichania, even herbivores could be aggressive. When he settled down for the night, he would not want to wake up to something nibbling on his toes.

Before George turned on the Hammer, he checked his *Charm*. The wrist computer gave off a signal that told the Hammer not to shoot him. One of the technicians at the lab said he was accidentally hit and it felt like being stung by a thousand wasps all at once. In any case, George hoped it would not fire a single pellet.

With his camp established, George strapped on the surge gun pack. The portable air compressor was lighter than he expected. It must be full of air, he mused. He pulled the satchel over his shoulder and headed deeper into the island. He had a few hours before sunset and wanted to explore. Maybe he could find the site that Vince thought was a campfire.

CHAPTER SEVEN

If George spent a little more time in the sub-cycle, he would have witnessed something incredible. Only minutes after he passed, about thirty feet below him, an Ichthyosaur gave birth. The squirming newborn floundered toward the surface for its first breath of air. The nurturing mother swam alongside it. Neither made it to the surface. An enormous dark figure rose from the depths, moving rapidly toward the mother and her newborn. It swallowed both of them whole. Princess Caroline and George would have been a light snack. Something sinister lurked in the deep dark and George had no idea.

Whatever animals inhabited this island beat a game trail leading inland. George decided to follow it to ease his journey. He did not want to fight through the thick undergrowth. The heat and humidity made the backpack feel heavy. He could feel sweat down the middle of his back, soaking his shirt. Along with the nutrient packs, George had two skinny bottles of purified water. He took off his backpack and sat under the shade of a large cycad plant. Before he knew it, he drank an entire bottle of water. He only had one left to last him until the morning. George suspected there had to be a fresh water source somewhere on the island. A trail like this, made by foraging animals, would ultimately lead to water. He reminded himself that the water source would also likely attract predators.

After a short rest, George strapped on his gear and started back along the trail. He watched small Pterosaurs swoop down from the forest canopy. They snatched large-winged insects out of the air as they darted between the trees. On one of the few occasions that George looked down at the ground, he noticed his boot had come unlaced. He leaned against a tree to tie it.

As he stepped away from the tree, George spied a large snake hanging on the limb directly where he was an instant ago. Its thick body suggested that this snake was a constrictor, much like a modern python or boa. Using the heat sensors in its nose, the snake must have spotted

George. It slowly moved toward him while he was distracted with his boot. If he had stopped here to rest or even tie both boots, he would have been wrapped up tight. George backed away from the snake. It slithered across the path and disappeared into the bushes. It had to be at least twenty feet long. George had an extreme fear of snakes like some people fear heights. Plenty of prehistoric creatures could make a meal out of him. He respected that. Snakes, however, scared the pants off him!

CRASH!

A loud sound that reminded George of a car crash broke the silence of the forest not long after he left the snake. George hurried down the path in the direction of the sound. Something moved in the grove ahead of him. Not wanting to be seen, he dropped down onto his hands and knees and crawled behind a large fern. From behind the fern, he could see a herd of Protoceratops in a clearing. Protoceratops, small cousins of Triceratops, had an armored shield that protected their head and neck. The little guys lacked the large brow horns though.

The two largest members of the group, apparently both males, faced each other with their heads lowered. They rushed at each other, crashed their armored heads together and then began to push. Obviously, they competed to see which one was the strongest. The winner would become the leader of the herd until a stronger male came along. Although Protoceratops were known to be small, George noticed that these seemed much smaller than he had expected. Maybe they looked small because of how far away he was. He tried to get a little closer by crawling on his stomach and got within fifteen yards. The entire herd focused on the two fighting males. This allowed him to get much closer. At this distance, he could easily see that, indeed, these Protoceratops were much smaller than the ones he had seen in museums.

Being this close to the herd gave George the opportunity to see something that he missed at first sight. Several tiny dinosaurs walked among the herd. These dinosaurs appeared to be about the size of a common housecat. The small things clambered in and out of a large nest. At first, George had no idea what he was seeing. Then he realized it was a community nest, a sort of rookery. He assumed the adult females took turns shepherding the dino-daycare. Seeing this suggested that dinos were more bird-like in caring for their young. Apparently they did not abandon them the way modern reptiles do, leaving the offspring to fend for themselves. This supported the hypothesis that some dinosaurs lived in a nesting ground. They probably never strayed far from home throughout their entire life cycle. Of course, in this case, being on an island limited their options. George knew that these Protoceratops were herbivores and relatively harmless. George thought he could maneuver past them and continue his search.

He continued walking deeper into the forest. He thought he was getting used to the forest sounds when he heard a limb snap. To his right something moved through the underbrush, and from the sound of it, it was relatively large. George hoped it was not another snake. He reached over his shoulder and unholstered the surge gun. He hoped he would not have to use it, but he decided that being safe was a priority. He listened for more activity and tried to get a fix on the direction from where it came. Maybe it was a stray Protoceratops, he thought. Through the undergrowth he could see more than one thing moving and each looked bigger than a Protoceratops. This time, George thought it would be better not to be too close. He ducked behind a tree, but not before inspecting its upper branches for dangling reptiles.

As the creatures pushed through the underbrush, George could now see that they were Hadrosaurs. These plant-eating dinosaurs are sometimes referred to as duckbills because of their flattened mouths that resembled the beak of a duck. Like the Protoceratops, George did not expect these Hadrosaurs to be so small. He guessed they might be juveniles. Then he saw tiny babies traveling among them as well. Things on the island seemed to grow in miniature. It became clear to George why the Protoceratops and these Hadrosaurs were so small. Animals living on islands must have to remain smaller than their cousins on the mainland. Since there is less food and water on an island, the animals do not have as much to eat or drink. Simply due to lack of resources, they could not grow as big. The Hadrosaurs appeared to be of the Bactrosaurus species. They should have been twenty feet long. Of the ones that passed by him now, the biggest could only be about four feet long.

As the herd approached, George continued to watch from behind the tree. The first few members walked right past him and did not even seem to know he was there.

Then one of the last adults happened to glance over and saw him. Although Bactrosaurus seemed to be a dinosaur species with no defenses, its tail could be a formidable weapon. Unlike a lizard's highly flexible tail, theirs were very stiff and rigid. They could swing them like oversized baseball bats. A hit from the tail of a large Hadrosaur would be enough to kill a grown man. Even these smaller versions would probably pack a powerful wallop. A direct hit might break George's arm or leg, if he was not careful.

Time seemed to stand still as George stared at the mini-Hadrosaurs and it stared back at him. Holding the surge gun in his hand, he began to slowly raise it. The Bactrosaurus leaned in very close to get a good look at him. The other herd members kept moving, now heading down the same trail George followed. The curious dino sniffed around him like some prehistoric puppy. It started sniffing his feet and then moved its flat beak all the way to George's head. With its face only inches away from his, a long sticky tongue slid out of its half-opened mouth and licked George across the face. It covered him with a slimy coating that smelled like half-eaten leaves. The Bactrosaurus apparently thought George tasted awful. It shook its head and spit at the ground. Some of the warm saliva splashed onto George's legs. George resisted the urge to gag. The Hadrosaur backed away and then trotted to catch up with the herd. George stood quietly. He did not want to attract any unnecessary attention, so he waited while the primordial ooze ran down his face, uncomfortably close to his mouth. If he could have screamed, he would have. It was the grossest thing that ever happened to him.

George did not move until the herd was out of sight. He watched the babies jump and play as their mothers tried to keep them in the center of the herd. Like children, these baby Hadrosaurs presumably had no idea of how dangerous life could be. All they seemed to care about was playing and having fun. Finally, George wiped the Hadro-slime from his face. He holstered the surge gun, glad he did not have to use it, and found a rag in his satchel. He thought of using one of the wide leafs behind him, but did not want to risk it being prehistoric poison ivy. Hopefully, he would not need the gun again. Maybe there are only herbivores on this island, he thought.

The shadows in the forest grew darker as the sun began to set. George could not go further into the island tonight. He needed enough daylight to make it safely back to camp. Thinking about the small dinos and the fact that he had only seen plant eaters, he felt a little foolish about the extreme defensive measures he took in setting up his camp. The *Hammer* would definitely sting a Protoceratops or adult Bactrosaurus, but it would do worse to one of the babies.

It made him a little nervous to be spending the night on the island. The rest of the team would be safe and warm inside the LV1. He knew he had to make sacrifices though. It was his uncle they were trying to find. He told Dr. Morgan early on that he wanted to be at the head of each mission, at least until they found Professor Stone. Now that George knew the island was somewhat safe, he looked forward to sleeping under the stars. He wondered how much the constellations changed in sixty-five million years. Could he spot Orion or the Big Dipper? A salty breeze blew in from the ocean. He decided the first priority would be to make a camp fire.

George had a lot to report. He wished he at least had a camera with him. It did not matter now, so he tried to relax. He let his mind wander to all of the unbelievable things he saw in only one day. He could not have anticipated it, but dropping his guard would prove to be a monumental mistake. Before sunset, he would no longer feel foolish about his excessive defense perimeter.

CHAPTER EIGHT

They came out of nowhere and attacked with lightning speed. George barely knew they were upon him before he felt the incredible sting as their teeth and claws ripped into his legs, back and neck. The creatures leapt through the air with their feet out in front of them and sliced through his clothing with their razor-sharp killing claws.

Struggling to regain his footing, George reached around and grabbed the creature that clawed at the back of his neck. It felt like a thick cluster of muscles covered in rough feathers. Squirming in his grip, he could not tell what it was. He pulled the tiny terror from his neck and hurled it over his shoulder. It landed on the ground about ten feet in front of him. Before the next one attacked, he got a good look at it. The shape and features seemed right, but the size was wrong. George familiarized himself with every known type of raptor. He had never studied one so small. The tiny raptor screamed as it regained its footing. This instantly sent the remaining pack members running in all directions. The swarm disappeared into the undergrowth.

George stood motionless, bloody and confused.

He tried to catch his breath and understand what happened. The last thing he remembered was walking back to camp thinking about the constellations and his friends safe in the LV1 command center. He thought about sending a report to Dr. Morgan. Then everything became a blur. A chirping bird rattled his focus. Normally, he liked to hear bird whistles. They always sounded musical to him. This one sounded shrill, not musical at all. Then he remembered that he heard this same chirping a moment before the attack.

The attack.

That chirping did not come from an evening bird singing a lullaby. It came from those vicious little dinos. George thought a moment about the one he pulled from his back. Could it have been a Tianyuraptor or Graciliraptor, he wondered. George dismissed that idea because these species lived in a much earlier time in the Cretaceous. He had the geography right, but his timing was off by several million years. He thought about the raptor and it seemed not much bigger than a common Blue Jay, but it did not fly. It jumped with ferocity though. The little raptor made him think again about the Blue Jay because of its fan of tail feathers. Royal blue covered most of its body, but it had white stripes on its wings and red tips to its tail feathers. George sarcastically thought *lucky me, I have possibly discovered a new species*. Unfortunately, the hungry raptors also discovered him.

But why did they stop the attack? George believed he knew the answer. Small raptors did not hunt like their larger cousins. Large raptors would likely rush in and attack until they finished the fight. The bone structure of these tiny raptors had to be too fragile to risk injury in a continued melee. Instead, they perfected the *slash-and-dash* method of hunting. They would ambush their prey, inflict as many small injuries as possible and then scurry away. This form of attack limited striking potential, but as the wounds accumulated, their prey slowly bled to death. He expected the pack to attack in wave after wave. If there were twenty or thirty of the little critters, they could cut him over one hundred times in less than a few minutes. Repeated attacks would make him too weak to fight back or escape. He suspected the next wave was about to start and the attacks would come faster after that.

The chirping continued on all sides. George knew they were circling him and communicating their next attack. His unseen attackers prepared for the next wave. He wanted to be ready. He grabbed the surge gun. If he could keep them at a distance, they could not slash him. He also started to jog in the direction of his camp. George did not risk a full out run. He did not want to excite the raptors or use all of his energy. He knew if he made it back to camp, the small dinosaurs did not stand a chance against the electro-net or the *Hammer*. The gun would rapidly pick off his attackers while avoiding him. George looked at his wrist to see the *Charm* that would keep him safe.

So much for reassuring himself. The *Charm* was gone. The only thing that kept the Hammer from also firing at him somehow fell off his wrist. He thought about where it could be. Did he lose it crawling on the ground to sneak up on the Protoceratops? Did the Bactrosaurus knock it off when it was sniffing him? Or did he lose it during the first wave of the raptor attack? It could be anywhere on the island. He could not risk going back to look for it. He knew without the sensor built into the *Charm*, the minute he set foot inside the perimeter, the fully automated gun would unleash its barrage of plastic pellets at him. The gun would not kill him, but it would leave him vulnerable to the raptors.

George decided his only chance of survival would be to ditch the camp and make a run for the sub-cycle. If he could make it to the beach, he could get back to the mainland and the LV1. He hated the idea of leaving the expensive equipment behind, but it was not worth losing his life. If something happened to him, then he would never find his uncle.

After a few minutes of silence, the telltale bird-like chirp broke the silence of the forest. This time George was ready for them. At least, he thought he was. They came at him from all sides. Some ran while others opened their wings and glided low to the ground. A few others, perched in the trees, glided down like fighter jets with teeth and claws. George pointed the surge gun at the largest group and fired. THWOMP. A massive thud came from the end of the barrel, followed by a huge cloud of dust on the ground. An instant ago, where there were raptors swarming on him, now he saw nothing but a few floating feathers drifting to the ground. The surge gun could knock down a charging rhino at close range. These mini-raptors never stood a chance. They literally disappeared from sight, thrown back fifty feet into the air. The sound of the gun caused the majority of the other raptors to flee in terror. Only a handful charged, oblivious to the potential danger for them.

The closest one approached George. It leaped toward him, hissing and screaming like a Spartan warrior, afraid of nothing. Using his satchel as a shield, George knocked the raptor to the ground. A second raptor sliced through his jeans, right above his ankle. George shook his leg, but the raptor would not let go. He kicked hard, like he was trying to score the winning field goal. The raptor lost its grip on his leg and went flying into the bushes. Individually, these little guys never stood a chance against George. As a group, however, they had the advantage. Once they regrouped, he would be in trouble.

A flash of light caught George's eye. The setting sun reflected off of something held by one of the raptors at the back of the pack. The *Charm*. It had George's *Charm* bracelet. It must have snatched it from him during the first assault. The dino seemed more interested in the device than its potential meal. If only George could get a hold of that raptor. He dared not fire the surge and launch both the raptor and the *Charm* into the underbrush. He would never find it then. After scattering the pack and fending off two attackers, he now hoped this one would charge him.

The lone raptor stared at George. It raised up on its toes, trying to make itself appear bigger, a gesture intended to intimidate its rival. The indicator on the surge gun showed that it had recharged. More of the pack gathered. George could feel trickles of blood on his arms and legs. He started to feel weak. The slash-and-dash technique worked amazingly well. George knew he had time to fire another surge blast into the pack. Maybe the shot would save his life, but maybe the pack would regroup. If he lost the *Charm*, he would definitely lose everything.

George found the knob that controlled the surge gun's intensity. He spun it to the lowest setting and aimed at the raptor holding his equipment. PHIST. The gun made a whisper sound. The blast hit the little raptor hard enough to knock it to the ground. Slightly dazed, it dropped the Charm. The quiet blast did not even startle the other raptors. Nine of them charged him. He had no time to think. George started yelling and ran directly toward them. As the raptors started to jump, George matched them. He managed to leap over his attackers and land on the sandy trail next to his Charm. He swatted away the dizzy thief and strapped his safety device to his wrist. The other raptors regrouped and headed back toward him. They leaped in unison. At the last second, George cranked the surge gun back up to maximum and fired at the oncoming wall of dinosaurs. THWOMP. The blast opened a hole in the wall and he scrambled through.

Running as fast as he could, the pain from the bites and scratches burned. It slowed him a little, but fear and survival instinct kept him moving. He did not look back. The raptors sounded too close. They no longer chirped. Now they screeched louder than their small bodies seemed capable.

George guessed the entire pack had to be behind him. He could not hear any sounds coming from in front or to the sides. He could see the camp ahead, but did not believe he could outrun the pack. His only chance would be one more blast. If he could scatter them again, he would have time to make it to safety. He checked to make sure that the surge gun had recharged. Then he jumped and spun backward at the same time. He wanted to increase the distance between him and the raptors while still being able to shoot. He felt like an action movie star. Flying through the air away from the pack, he fired.

PHIST.

George hit the ground hard. The backpack dug into his spine. The surge gun did not even slow the onslaught. Somehow he managed to switch the gun back to its lowest setting. A full charge would have stunned the whole pack. Now thirty or more raptors swelled at his feet. Feeling pain all over his body, George could only cover his head with his arms before the final strike. As claws and teeth dug into his body, he thought of his uncle and Parker. He would never see them again. He failed them all.

Then suddenly, the pain stopped. Something else caught the raptors' attention. George lowered his arms and opened his eyes. Dangling from a nearby branch, an enormous snake gobbled one of the raptors. The other pack members turned to fight this new threat. George crawled backwards on his elbows, watching the spectacle. The large snake moved faster than he would have liked. It wrapped up three raptors in its coils as it finished swallowing the first. The others started biting and slicing at its long body. George thought a moment about the irony of his least favorite animal being the one to save him. Then he realized he should be running.

Although his injuries were not life threatening, the blood loss could be dangerous if he could not stop the attacks. He ran from the battle, stumbling along the way. He could feel the strength in his body slowly draining. One more attack would be big trouble. Catching his breath, he made sure the surge gun was set back to maximum. If another attack came, he could be ready.

George limped along, constantly checking for followers. The giant snake must have kept them occupied. Still, if any of the raptors survived, they would likely track their weakened prey. He needed to make it to the electro-net perimeter. Then he could activate it with his *Charm*. Then he could bandage his wounds and rest without fear of another attack.

Only twenty meters to the camp and George found the walk extremely difficult. He felt dizzy and his legs ached. Then he noticed something else. The raptors started following him again. They did not hide in the bushes. They walked along the path, but they stayed out of range of the surge gun. He thought about how smart they seemed. They must learn and adapt fast. Instead of risking another blast, they would wait for him to fall. He realized the snake must have won the other fight, or they would not need to be following this potential meal. Each time George stopped to catch his breath, the pack stopped. They were in no hurry. They lived and hunted on this island. They had nowhere else to go. This was their island. Darkness closed in around George. Once night took over, he had no chance of survival unless he could make it to camp.

CHAPTER NINE

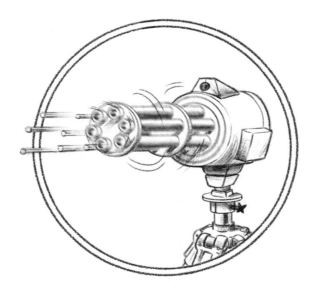

"Talk to me George," Parker called. Her voice sounded tiny coming through the *Charm*.

"I'm here," he answered.

Parker took a moment to respond. When she did, her voice sounded shaky. She must have been worried about him. She said, "We lost your vital signs for a few minutes. I thought something happened to you. What's going on?"

"Some of the locals invited me to dinner."

"What are you talking about?" interrupted Vince's voice. George could picture him standing over Parker's shoulder at the console.

George said, "The only problem was they wanted me to be the main course. I dropped my *Charm*, but I have it back now. Don't worry. I'll see you in the morning. George out."

Almost as soon as he signed off, the ground began to rumble. Ever so slightly, the noise started low and rapidly became quite loud. The vibrations even shook dry leaves off the nearby trees. They fell like miniature paratroopers dropping in on their target.

Behind him, George saw the raptors freeze. They looked confused, not sure whether to attack of flee. Further behind them, George saw the cause of the tremors. The herd of Bactrosaurus charged down the trail. Even at four feet long, each weighed nearly two hundred and fifty pounds. That weight multiplied by about thirty herd members practically caused a localized earthquake. George had plenty of time to jump clear, but the tiny raptors met with an unpleasant surprise. George could not see for sure, but he did not think any of the vicious pack survived.

"Yeehaw!" cheered George as the last of the Bactrosaurus stampeded past him. The rumbling gradually faded as they headed off to some other part of the island. He saw no sign of his hunters. He thought how cool it was that plant-eating duckbills saved him. The victory gave George a boost of adrenaline. His wounds stopped hurting, at least, temporarily. George laughed at his outburst. He felt bad about getting angry with the duckbill that licked his face earlier. He probably owed them his life. A slimy dino kiss was a small price to pay.

With only feet to go to the safety of his camp, George had a nagging curiosity. What caused the Hadros to stampede in the first place, he wondered. He mused that maybe they liked him. The grin that started with his victory yell instantly faded. He looked back to see something picking over the remains of the small raptors. Even in the fading daylight, George could still see the yellow head with the red line running down the back of the neck. This Velociraptor stopped chewing and looked up at him with its one left eye.

"Lefty," said George.

Lefty answered with a screech. The other two six foot raptors stopped their snacking and looked to Lefty. Apparently, they had no problem swimming to the island. The jumbled display when they chased Vince must have been frantic. Obviously, when they were not specifically chasing something, they could swim the long distance. They probably came to hunt the smaller Bactrosaurus. On the island, they could likely capture their prey one on one. Now Lefty had George in his sights.

He slowly raised the surge gun. George aimed at Lefty. He thought if he stopped the leader, the other two might flee. He said, "I hope it was worth your swim."

Lefty tilted his head to the side, apparently trying to understand what George was doing. George checked the intensity setting. Then he squeezed the trigger. The maximum blast knocked all three raptors to the ground. Lefty rolled head over tail. George turned to run. If the raptors were unconscious, they would not be for long.

George did not realize how much the encounter with the mini-raptors wore on him. His adrenaline rush faded and he quickly ran out of energy. If only he could make it the last several feet before Lefty and his friends recovered. George checked over his shoulder. Lefty already recovered. He nudged one of the other raptors with his snout. George turned to run and tripped over a thick tree branch. He fell hard on the surge gun. It made a strange crunching sound.

Lefty saw George on the ground and broke into a full run. George tried to crawl toward the electro-net perimeter. He could probably reach one of the units if he stretched out his hand. Lefty closed the distance in a matter of seconds. George rolled toward him and pointed the surge gun. He pulled the trigger.

Nothing happened.

The trigger snapped off in his hand. Now he understood what the crunching sound was. Lefty, apparently, did not know the gun was broken. The one-eyed raptor cut to the side and disappeared into the ferns. George took an instant to marvel at how fast the Velociraptor learned. It must have recognized the shape of the gun and remembered what it could do. He did not think Lefty would give up, but he probably would not be so direct in his next attack.

It would be easier to drop the surge gun pack. In his weakened state, George could only crawl the last few feet. Maybe the raptors feared the gun, but if they were as smart as George suspected, he would have to fire it again soon to keep them away. If he did not shoot, they would likely understand that he was defenseless. George kept the pack with him and scooted toward the perimeter.

Looking at the ground, George did not waste any energy checking for followers. He felt exhausted and dizzy. He could not make it much farther. Now, instead of leaves and little rocks, George saw a pair of feet directly in front of him. He could not mistake those overgrown chicken legs, each equipped with those sinister killing claws. He looked up slowly into Lefty's one good eye. The raptor sniffed him. George felt the other two sniffing and poking at his sides. Lefty lowered his head and breathed deep. Then he stood as tall as he could and shrieked out a victory roar.

George kept moving. He saw Lefty's killing claw dangerously close to his face. Still, the raptors did not strike. None of them delivered the final blow, yet they never left his side. George could see that he was now inside the perimeter of the electro-net. If he activated it now, the raptors would be trapped inside with him. This would make them all the more dangerous. He knew a threatened animal could act unpredictably.

"What are you waiting for, you over-sized parrot?" screamed George.

The raptors hissed. As their hissing died out, another sound replaced it. At first, it reminded him of the click, click, click of baseball cards on a bicycle wheel. The new noise increased in speed and volume until it sounded like the longest, loudest cat purr he ever heard. George looked up to see wide palm leaves suddenly cut in half. The raptors squealed in pain.

The *Hammer*!

One of his attackers must have moved in range of the *Hammer*. The mini-gun spun into action. It fired thousands of rounds that shredded plant life and stung the Velociraptors. George kept his head down as the *Hammer* did its job. Lefty and his friends dashed into the forest in separate directions. Once clear of the infrared sensor, the life-saving weapon slowed to a stop.

George achingly turned onto his back. Safe, and alone, inside the perimeter, he tapped a button on his *Charm* and the electro-net whirred to life. Then he fainted.

He awoke some time later. He could not tell how long he slept, but it was still dark. George turned on a small flashlight. He looked at the cuts on his arms. The bleeding had stopped. He did not feel as woozy. Then he checked the *Hammer's* ammo supply. It looked over half full. If Lefty came back, he would get a nasty surprise. George spent a few minutes to do some first aid. Then he ate two of the nutrient packs. He did not realize how hungry he was until he licked the inside of the tinfoil wrapper.

With the electro-net turned on and the *Hammer* at the ready, George felt like he could relax for a minute. He decided not to call the LV1. They could not help him right now, so he did not want to worry them. He did not like the idea of spending the night with Lefty, but a run to the beach would be too dangerous. The moon and stars gave some light. However, a predator like Lefty would have the advantage in a nighttime attack. Besides, if his uncle spent the night on this island, then he could.

George wondered how Professor Stone would have dealt with Lefty, especially since he did not have the *Hammer* or even a surge gun. He never found the remains of the campfire that Vince spotted on the interactive map. Maybe it was a coincidence, some rocks that happened to land in a circle after a storm or Hadrosaur stampede. Maybe his uncle never even came here. They were, after all, dealing with time travel. His uncle could have gone anywhere and they had no way to track him.

In the morning, George felt much better. He had a few hours of uninterrupted sleep. Lefty and his soldiers did not come back. The *Hammer* did not fire and the electro-net did not spark once. This gave George a false sense of security. He knew the raptors had to be out there. Maybe they went for reinforcements. Or maybe they found an unsuspecting Protoceratops for a midnight snack. In either case, George kept a watchful eye as he packed his gear. He did not want to leave anything behind for future paleontologists to discover. He kept the *Hammer* activated until the last possible moment.

CHAPTER TEN

Packing took longer than he wanted. George tried to be as quiet as possible. Quiet meant slow. He used valuable time fitting things back into the two metal cases. He knew Lefty could be back at any minute. Something moved in the bushes behind him. He wanted nothing more than to be off this island.

George practically tiptoed down to the beach. The cuts on his arms left him feeling achy. They made it hard to carry the supplies. He sat them down on the beach, still damp from morning dew. The humidity caused a low fog that kept him from seeing the mainland.

Something over there bellowed. The echo carried eerily through the fog. George deftly opened the sub-cycle and slid the two cases in place. He stretched for a moment and looked back at the island. It seemed peaceful. However, George knew its real dangers.

Parker's voice shattered the quiet. "George. Come in, George."

George slapped his hand over the *Charm*. He tried to muffle the sound.

Too late.

The three Velociraptors must have been watching him the whole time. As soon as they heard Parker calling for him, they stepped out of the underbrush at the edge of the beach. They did not run or attack. They simply stood watching him.

George whispered back to Parker, "I can't talk right now."

She ignored him. "Listen. We miscalculated. We have less than an hour before the LV1 goes back through the *Goal*. You have to get back here now!"

That's what I'm trying to do, he wanted to shout. Somehow, he managed to remain calm. He did not want to make any sudden movements that would bring the raptors down on top of him. George slowly stepped into the sub-cycle. He reached for the hatch to pull down over his head. Suddenly, Lefty charged. George sealed the hatch an instant before Lefty's snapping jaws reached him. He did not think the raptors could chew through Princess Caroline's waterproof exterior. Still, he would not take that chance. George hit all of the switches and peeled out on the wet clay. The sub-cycle spun in a full circle, then he was facing the water. George shoved the throttle forward and splashed into the sea.

"I'm on my way." George took a moment to respond to Parker. He had nothing more to say at the moment. Then he checked the sonar. It confirmed his fear. The raptors followed him. He knew they had to swim on the surface. They would not be able to dive down deep like he could. There was no way their skinny legs could match the speed of his engine either. He could easily beat them to the opposite shore, but he would only have a narrow lead. They might catch him before the rear door of the LV1 fully opened. His friends would be defenseless, unless he warned them.

Princess Caroline sent vibrations through the water that George could not see or detect. However, one creature in the depths did sense them. Tiny receptors lined its body. That was how it located its prey in the deep dark water. The massive shape moved instinctively toward the sub-cycle.

George tried to call the LV1. "Parker, can you read me?"

No response.

"Parker. Vince. Anybody? I am on my way, but do not open the back door. I repeat – do not. We have some uninvited guests that I will have to get rid of first."

Again, no response. George figured his radio signal could not transmit from so far below the water. He would try again back on land. He hoped that would not be too late. Then George noticed a new signal on his sonar. Something came directly toward him. He double-checked to see the raptors falling behind. In a few seconds, George would have visual contact with the new creature.

It turned out to be not one, but four Plesiosaurs. He recognized their long flippers, although these had to be adolescents, not much bigger than the sub-cycle. He thought maybe the harmless sea creatures were coming to investigate him. They did not slow or give him a second glance as they passed. They moved up toward the surface, probably to refill their lungs with air. He watched on the sonar as they reacted to the unexpected raptors. It looked like an air stunt show. Four blips headed toward the other three and then suddenly split off in different directions. George tried to get a look through the view portal, but he was too deep and the water too murky. He wondered if they were escaping from something.

Distracted by the Plesiosaurs, George did not notice another new reading on the sonar. This red dot looked bigger than any of the other combined. It came up slowly. If George had been paying attention, he would have realized that it was the same digital signature he saw several times before. This hunter came close to Vince the first time they encountered Lefty. It tracked Princess Caroline's vibrations and it came hungry.

At the last second, George looked forward. He saw a dark shape fill his vision. He hit the switch for the underwater spotlight. It gleamed on a double row of countless razor sharp teeth. The light must have temporarily blinded the creature. It dove beneath him. This gave George a chance to see it, before its wake sent the sub-cycle into a barrel roll.

Tylosaurus!

A member of the Mosasaur family, this giant swimming reptile was among the most feared creatures in the sea. It was big enough to attack anything that entered their watery world without fear. Tyrannosaurus may have been the *king* on land, but Tylosaurus ruled the sea!

George watched the sonar to see where the Tylosaurus went. The monster dwarfed him. If it decided to attack, he did not think Princess Caroline would stand a chance. Maybe the Tylosaurus could not figure out what kind of creature George was. The oceans produced countless creatures with unusual and dangerous survival capabilities. Maybe the predator wanted to know what it was up against before it struck. The Tylosaurus circled beneath him, but George kept moving forward. If he could make it to the beach, then he would only have the Velociraptors to worry about.

Then the big red blip disappeared from his screen. It must have dived so deep to be out of range. Was it leaving? Was it preparing for an attack? George had no idea what to expect. Suddenly, the red dot reappeared on the sonar. It looked to be directly beneath him. George braced for impact. He did not think the sub-cycle could withstand the crushing pressure of the Tylosaurus's massive jaws. He could not take his eyes off the computer screen. He watched the blip closing on him, then it changed direction ever so slightly.

The Tylosaurus angled away from Princess Caroline. Apparently, the three smaller figures treading water on the surface proved to be an easier target. The Tylosaurus rushed past George. Where there were three raptor signals a moment ago, George now only saw one on his radar. The Tylosaurus gobbled up two of the predators. It swam in a huge arc and then snatched the third one, pulling it down into the depths.

"So long, Lefty," George said to himself.

A moment later, the Tylosaurus returned. Could it still be hungry, he wondered. Maybe it needed to prove to anything in its water who was boss. The mighty creature did not attack the sub. It swam past, missing by mere inches. George knew he had to be getting close to the beach. The Tylosaurus would be unable to follow him on land. He guided the sub-cycle down into the shallow water. He hoped the thick seaweed would hide him there. He turned sideways and could see the Tylosaurus floating near the surface. Like most sea-going dinosaurs, it needed air and paused for a breath.

The beast continued to swim in the area, so George waited. He did not want to risk attracting it. He had no idea if it was looking for him or simply exercising after its Velociraptor meal. George sat in the sub-cycle, ten feet below the surface and hidden by swaying seaweed. Almost thirty minutes passed. George started to worry if he would run out of oxygen. He did not remember from his training that Princess Caroline had gills. Of course, they were not really fish gills, but high-tech filters that could take oxygen out of the water. He would not run out of air.

But he was running out of time!

When he left the island, Parker told him he had less than an hour before the LV1 did its automatic return. If he was not safe inside, he would be stranded in the past exactly like his uncle. George could not wait any longer. He sped along the sea floor. The sub-cycle's wheels stirred up sand into the water. This got the Tylosaurus's attention. It bore down on him like a fifty foot long torpedo.

At the last second, George remembered one of Princess Caroline's security features. He wished he paid more attention during training. It did not matter now. George hit a button that released a non-toxic chemical into the water. It surrounded the sub-cycle in an inky cloud like an octopus. The chemical stung the sensitive receptors on the nose of the Tylosaurus. The king of the sea did an underwater backflip and swam away like a scolded puppy. The chemical dissolved quickly, so George wasted no time getting to the beach.

As soon as he made it on dry land, he hit the communicate button on his *Charm*. He knew he no longer had to worry about a raptor chase. "Open the door. I'm almost there!" He could barely keep from yelling. He was almost out of time. That made him extremely anxious. George reached the ramp a second after it hit the ground. The wet wheels skidded on the metal floor of the LV1 when he hit the brakes. He almost ran into Vince, but the chief of security held out his arms to keep him safe.

George could hear Parker yelling to Lloyd, "Close the door. We only have five minutes."

George climbed out of the sub-cycle. He could feel himself shaking. He must be having an adrenaline surge. How much adrenaline could one body make in twenty-four hours, he wondered. That would be a question for Sonya and it would keep until later. George tried to catch his breath.

Parker pushed past Vince and wrapped George in a big hug. She said, "I was so…I mean, you had us all pretty scared. New rule: no more sleep-overs on Raptor Island."

Vince said, "Would you like to do the honors?"

He handed George a microphone. He knew they were supposed to send a report before they activated the time travel. It would be a one-way message. Dr. Morgan had no way to send a response back in time, but their message would go forward. George thought about what he would say. It occurred to him that whatever he said was probably already saved in that secret file on Dr. Morgan's computer. He was scared to go on this adventure at first, but he felt like he gained some confidence. He wanted to tell about the Sauropods feeding their young by knocking over trees. The thought of using the EB5 to trick the Saichania made him smile. He could probably fill a book with his experiences at the place Parker called Raptor Island. Being the first human to see a living dinosaur stunned him, but somehow it was not enough. Despite his best efforts, they saw no sign of Professor Stone. George hoped he would rescue his uncle on their very first trip. Maybe it was a silly idea. He suspected, judging from the number of files on Dr. Morgan's computer, that they would have many more adventures. And he believed he would see his uncle again.

George decided what he would say. He came up with a name for his team that he thought sounded pretty cool. He said, "The Paleonauts are ready to come home." Then he added, "Sorry, this is George...I mean Dinosaur George."

PALEOFACTS

Nemegtosaurus (*pronounced: NEH-meg-tuh-SAWR-us*) means Nemgt Lizard. Found in Mongolia, Nemegtosaurus is related to Diplodocus. It was a member of the Sauropod family that used its height to reach leaves that were too high for other herbivores.

QUADRAPEDAL HERBIVORE
HEIGHT: 23 FEET (7 METERS)
LENGTH: 50 FEET (15.2 METERS)
PERIOD: LATE CRETACEOUS (ABOUT 100 TO 66 MILLION YEARS AGO)

Saichania (*pronounced: sye-CHAY-nee-ah*) means beautiful one. Saichania fossils were found in southern Mongolia with much of its armor plating still in position. Like other Ankylosaurs, it had a bony club on the end of its tail and tis neck, back and stomach were covered by rows of spikes and knobs of bony plates.

QUADRAPEDAL HERBIVORE
HEIGHT: 8 FEET (2.4 METERS)
LENGTH: 23 FEET (7 METERS)
PERIOD: LATE CRETACEOUS

Velociraptor (*pronounced: veh-loss-ih-RAP-tor*) means quick plunderer or rapid robber. Found in Mongolia, China and Russia, Velociraptor was a ferocious predator with the second toe of each foot bearing an oversized, recurved claw. Known as the "killing claw", they used it to slash its prey. Velociraptor may have hunted in packs when attacking larger prey.

BIPEDAL CARNIVORE
HEIGHT: 2.5 FEET (0.8 METERS)
LENGTH: 5.9 FEET (1.8 METERS)
PERIOD: LATE CRETACEOUS

Plesiosaurus (*pronounced: PLEE-see-uh-SAWR-us*) was a fast swimming reptile with four large flippers and an elongated neck. They used their necks to catch fish and other small aquatic creatures. Plesiosaurs may have been able to come on land and lay eggs, like modern sea turtles.

LENGTH: 23 FEET (7 METERS)
WEIGHT: 3 TONS
PERIOD: LATE CRETACEOUS

Protoceratops (*pronounced: pro-toe-SAIR-uh-tops*) means first horned face. Protoceratops were small cousins of Triceratops, the giant three-horned dinosaurs of North America. Protoceratops lacked the horns of its larger cousin, but still had a formidable weapon in its beak-like jaws and armor protected skull. The frill of the skull may have acted as a shield to protect its vulnerable neck.

QUADRAPEDAL HERBIVORE
HEIGHT: 2.6 FEE (0.8 METERS)
LENGTH: 6 FEET (1.8 METERS)
PERIOD: LATE CRETACEOUS

Bactrosaurus (*pronounced: BAK-truh-SAWR-us*) means Bactrian lizard. Bactrosaurus is one of the earliest known duck-billed Hadrosaurs. It had fewer teeth than later Hadrosaurs. These plant eating dinosaurs lived in small herds and probably migrated each year. The island members would have remained much smaller than those who lived on the mainland.

BIPEDAL HERBIVORE
HEIGHT: 8 FEET (2.4 METERS)
LENGTH: 20 FEET (6.1 METERS)
PERIOD: LATE CRETACEOUS

Mini Island Raptor has not been given an official name yet. It was smaller than a housecat, but was equipped with the same terrible weapons that its larger mainland cousins had. Although this dinosaur appears small, its sharp teeth and claws made it one of the most deadly of island inhabitants.

BIPEDAL CARNIVORE
HEIGHT: 1 FOOT (0.3 METERS)
LENGTH: 2 FEET (0.6 METERS)
PERIOD: LATE CRETACEOUS

Tylosaurus (*pronounced: TIE-low-SAWR-us*) was a member of the Mosasaur family. These creatures lived at the time of the dinosaurs, but are not a part of the dinosaur family. They are considered swimming reptiles. These huge aquatic reptiles were among the most feared animals of the seas. With their snake-like bodies, large flippers and a second row of teeth in their upper jaw, few animals would survive an encounter with a Tylosaurus.

LENGTH: 50 FEET (15.2 METERS)
WEIGHT: 20 TONS
PERIOD: LATE CRETACEOUS

AFTERWORD

As a child I dreamed of traveling back in time to see living dinosaurs. As an adult, I've dreamed of creating a story that would allow children to use their imaginations to travel back to age of dinosaurs. Dinosaur George and the Paleonauts has given me the chance to fulfill both dreams!

Since 1997, I've traveled throughout North America, teaching children about paleontology. In that time, I've performed to over 2 million students and made many new friends along the way. It's been a wonderful journey. But I never could have done it without the support of my family and friends.

I would like to dedicate this first book to my parents, Lyle and Elizabeth, as well as Mark, Cindy, Lisa, Jay, Leslie, Jared, Josh and the light of my life, my niece Caroline. My family has been my inspiration and has always supported me in everything I do. Without their help, I could have never accomplished the things I've done over the years.

I would also like to recognize my friends Don Taylor, Chip Davis, Dave Eisenstein, and David Boswell who have worked so hard to help me along the way. And a special thank you to Ron "Tinker" Frithiof who has helped me more than I can every repay. His friendship, guidance and support have helped me weather every storm.

And finally, I would like to say thank you to Mark Miller. This book may never have been published if it weren't for Mark. He is an incredible writer and has been a great partner in this project. I look forward to working with him on many future books.

Dinosaur George

MEET THE AUTHORS

Dinosaur George Blasing is a self-taught paleontologist and animal behaviorist with more than 35 years of study and research. Blasing is a public speaker, writer and television personality who has performed live to over 2 million people and has lectured in over 2800 museums, schools and public events. With the addition of his latest program, Museum in the Classroom, he is now able to bring an entire museum to the schools he visits. www.DinosaurGeorge.com or www.Facebook.com/DinosaurGeorgeFanPage

Mark Miller currently resides in Florida with his wife and four children. Mark has written numerous novels, screenplays, short stories and digital series. He has geared his fantasy series, *The Empyrical Tales*, for the classroom and explored his spirituality, writing both with his father and daughter. He also created the young reader series *Ask DG* based on Dinosaur George's popular YouTube series. Inspirational stories with positive messages are his goal with everything he writes.
www.MillerWords.com or www.Facebook.com/MarkMillerAuthor

MEET THE ILLUSTRATOR

Gabriel Bush has been drawing for as long as he can remember. As a child, his main subject matter was superheroes, from Superman to Spiderman to anything else that popped into his head. As an adult, that hasn't changed much—superheroes of every shape and form remain a favorite subject matter—although there is nothing he does not enjoy illustrating. Gabriel lives in Texas with his beautiful wife and two girls, where he continues to hone his love of art. Whether he is using pencil and paper, chalk, airbrush, or the computer to create art, he thanks God every day for the ability to create something out of nothing. www.GabeBush-art.tumblr.com or www.Facebook.com/GabeBush.FanPage

Made in the USA
Columbia, SC
25 July 2021